MADDOX

SAVAGE KINGS MC

LANE HART

D.B. WEST

COPYRIGHT

Edited by All About the Edits
Cover by Marianne Nowicki www.PremadeEbookCoverShop.com
Photo by Andrei Vishnyakov
https://www.instagram.com/vishstudio/
Model Anthony Maximoff
https://www.instagram.com/anthony_maximoff/

WARNING: THIS BOOK IS NOT SUITABLE FOR ANYONE UNDER 18. PLEASE NOTE THAT IT CONTAINS VIOLENT SCENES THAT MAY BE A TRIGGER FOR INDIVIDUALS WHO HAVE BEEN IN SIMILAR SITUATIONS.

PROLOGUE

Maddox Holmes
Six years ago...

MOST BIRTHDAYS ARE THE SAME OLD SHIT. THEY COME AND GO without you feeling any differently than the day before, despite being an entire year older.

My fifteenth birthday on the other hand was a game changer, and not just because I was going to get my learner's permit.

"Good luck. I'm sure you'll do great," my mother says with a quick hug before she shoves a manila folder toward my chest. "Everything you need is in here. Just hand the whole thing over to the officer."

"Okay, Mom." I take the folder from her and follow the DMV official down the hall to her small, messy office.

"Have a seat so we can finish up your paperwork, then get you started on your written exam."

"Sure," I happily agree before I plop my ass down in the chair across from her desk.

"Do you have your two proofs of identification and proof of residency?"

"Yep, got that all right here," I say before I squeeze the metal clasp to open the folder and start pulling out the documents my mom put together for me. I grab the small white and blue piece of paper first. "Here's my social security card."

Then, I go for the thickest piece of paper, my birth certificate. Since I've never actually seen it before, I lower my eyes to look it over while the agent scans my social security card. It's pretty cool seeing today's date on there, just fifteen years ago...

"Who the fuck is Deacon Fury?" I exclaim when I see the unfamiliar and unusual name.

"Excuse me?" the DMV agent asks with an arched eyebrow.

"Sorry, nothing," I tell her before reading the man's name again, then the title underneath that says, "Child's Father."

I swear it feels like the tiny room starts to spin around me. My father's name, the man who has raised me for the past fifteen years, even if he did a shitty job most of the time, is Todd Holmes.

"Do you have your birth certificate?" the agent asks, snapping me out of my vertigo.

"Ah, yeah. Here." I hold the paper out to her.

"Hmm," she says when she reads it. "These have two different names."

"What?" I ask.

"Do you have any other paperwork?"

"I...I dunno," I state, while staring at her in confusion. "Here." I offer her the entire folder, since I can't seem to do much more than blink at the moment.

"Ah, here's your Change of Name form."

"My *what*?" I ask.

"Change of name," she says, holding up the documents in her hand. "Your parents changed your name from Maddox Fury to Maddox Holmes when you were just a few weeks old."

When my jaw falls open, she adds, "You didn't know that?"

I shake my head because the ability to speak has left me.

My parents changed my name?

And my father is...not my father?

What kind of alternate universe did I step into? Is she pranking me right now?

"Could I...could I see those again?" I ask, snatching the paperwork from her hand instead of waiting for her response.

"Are you okay?" the officer asks while I read over the official Change of Name form that has everything she just said written out. I'm not Maddox Holmes. I was born Maddox fucking Fury.

"Should we do this another day?" she asks, while I continue staring at the words as if expecting them to suddenly shift around on the page and make more sense.

"Ah, yeah. I'll, um, I'll come back," I tell her as I get up from my chair, still holding the form, and start toward the door.

"Wait! Here are your other documents," she says.

I take them from her, then sit down in the hallway outside of her door and reread them a hundred times. My emotions switch from confusion, to anger at my mother for not telling me, to...relief. I'm relieved that Todd is not my dad, he's just asshole Todd. We're not related, which is sort of a miracle, because deep down, I've never liked him. As for Todd, well, even when I was just a kid, I thought he hated me. I'm starting to realize that he really did. He hates me because I'm not his son, but he's had to pretend to give a shit about me for fifteen fucking years.

Being free of him feels great. Only now, there's this gaping hole inside me where that asshole used to be, and I don't have any clue who belongs in it other than his name—Deacon Fury.

Deacon. He sounds like a badass, much more so than Todd. Fucking Todd. I never met anyone with that name that I liked. My father—no, my stepfather—completely ruined the name.

"You can't sit here," a guy in a wrinkled suit and combover says to me.

"Okay, I'm going," I reply before I shove all the documents inside the envelope and get to my feet, ready to finally face my mother and get some damn answers.

"How did it go?" she asks with a smile when she stands up in the chair and comes over to meet me.

"I didn't take the test," I tell her.

"Well, why not?"

"Because there was some confusion over who the hell I am!" I yell at her.

"Wh-what are you talking about?" she asks, her eyes cutting around the crowded waiting room, probably searching for any of her uppity friends who may have overheard my outburst.

"Who the fuck is Deacon? And why didn't you tell me he's my father?" I shout at her, not caring who hears.

"Maddox!" my mother hisses at me before she grabs me by my elbow and leads me out of the office. On the sidewalk out front, she stops and then has the nerve to tell me, "It doesn't matter."

I blink at her in disbelief at her brush-off before I repeat those same words aloud. "It doesn't matter? *It doesn't matter* who my father is? Maybe not to you, but it matters a whole fucking lot to me, Mom!"

"Maddox, calm down and watch your language! This is not the time nor the place—"

"It's not?" I interrupt to ask. "Then when *is* a good time and place? You've had fifteen fucking years to tell me, and you haven't found your moment yet?"

"I'm sorry, okay?" she says as her prim and proper posture starts to deflate.

"Who is Deacon? Does he even know that I exist?" I ask, since it's the first I've heard of him.

My mother shakes her head and then crosses her arms over her chest. "I never told him because we knew it would only cause problems…"

"We?" I ask. "You mean you and *Todd?*"

"Yes. You have to put yourself in his shoes. Your father and I met while I was pregnant. Todd married me right after you were born. He agreed to raise you as his son but didn't want to deal with having another man in our life..."

"He's not my father!" I shout at her. "And you kept my real father from me to make Todd happy? What the fuck is wrong with you? Do you even know where this other man is so that I can find him and tell him that I'm his son?"

She looks away before she answers so softly I almost miss it. "He's dead."

"What?" I ask as a heavy boulder settles into my gut.

"If I knew he was sick, I would've told you. He died of lung cancer."

"Would you have really told me, Mom? Or would you have kept on lying to me every fucking day?" I bark at her, still not entirely sure if I believe her when she says he's dead. "When? When did he die? Before I was born?" I ask, wanting more details. *Deserving* more details. I deserve to know every fucking thing about the man who makes up half of me.

"A year or so ago," she responds, which only floors me even more

"So, I missed meeting my father by a year? Fourteen years, you could've told us both and you didn't, so now I'll never meet him! How could you do this to me?"

"I'm sorry, Maddox. We did what we thought was best..."

"No," I say, cutting her off. "You did what *Todd* thought was best for *him*, not me! He's always hated my guts and I guess now I know why. He made me think I wasn't ever good enough for him because I'm *nothing* but a reminder of another man you were with before him! I've *never* been his son and I never will be!"

The anger I've made myself keep bottled up inside me for years chooses that moment to burst free. No, it's more than anger, it's pure rage. Fucking Todd is about to get a shitload of payback by way of my fists pounding into his face.

Screw him, his money and his life. I'd rather have nothing and the truth than all the money in the world and living a lie.

CHAPTER ONE

Maddox
Present day...

TEENAGERS HAVE ENOUGH PROBLEMS TRYING TO FIGURE OUT who they are. Throw in the added complication of having a part of me, half of me, that I knew nothing about and I nearly went insane on my fifteenth birthday.

The night I learned the truth, I beat the living shit out of Todd. He was so badly injured that he and my mom sent me away to military school for the next two years.

After I graduated, I couldn't go back home. I had to leave, to search for the answers about who my real father was so I could finally find myself.

That's why I set off on my own without a penny to my name when I was eighteen.

A search of the internet brought me to Emerald Isle and the Savage Kings MC, thanks to the memorial page for my father on their website. I figured if anyone knew who Deacon Fury really was, it would be these guys, since he was their founder and former president.

But once I was there and found out the current president and VP were my family, I couldn't find the words to own up to who I was. Hell, I didn't really know myself. So, I kept my mouth shut and listened and watched them, hoping to learn about the man I'd never get a chance to know.

It turned out the brothers in the MC were cool as fuck. I didn't just want to know my relatives, I wanted to be one of them. I needed to become a Savage King. It was the only thing I had been certain of in my life.

The one person who found out my secret was Reece, the MC's computer genius. He dug into my history when I was finally nominated to become a prospect. He took me aside after he did my background search and asked me about the name I was born with. I told him the truth and begged him to keep my secret. Not to deceive anyone in the club, but because I wanted to earn my patch on my own merits, not because of the man who unknowingly made me.

Thankfully, Reece agreed. He's kept his mouth shut after I assured him I wasn't here to make a claim to my father's estate, the MC, or anything else I hadn't earned.

And my sponsor, War, well, he took me in off the streets and was a helluva lot nicer to me than Todd ever was, without knowing anything but my second name. Over the last few years, War began to fill the place of the father I wish I had and the father I'll never meet. He and the other brothers in the MC have made me feel like I've finally found the place where I belong.

So, whenever War calls, like right now, you better believe I fucking jump.

I toss down the hammer in my hand to pull my untraceable flip phone from my pocket.

"Yes, sir?" I answer when I quickly put the burner phone up to my ear.

"Where are you? Are you still on the island?" War asks, the usually calm man sounding frantic.

"Yeah, I'm just finishing boarding up the Jolly Roger, and then I'm gonna get inland."

"Good. Great. I need you to do me a favor."

"Sure," I respond.

"I'm tied up, so I need you to take the club's van and get your ass down to Wilmington to pick up my sister—"

"You have a sister too?" I ask in surprise. I've known the man for almost four years and he's never once mentioned her. Which isn't that surprising, I guess. War barely talked about his son before the whole Child Protective Services mess.

"Yeah, I have a sister, Audrey O'Neil," he replies. "She goes to school at Westchester in Wilmington, and she lives in the Chatham apartments, number two-twenty-eight B. Got all that?"

"Yes," I tell him, repeating it over and over again in my head so I won't forget it until I have some pen and paper.

"Whatever it takes, get her inland, at least west to Raleigh or Cary, and keep her safe. She should have credit cards to pay for a hotel if you're low on cash. Do this for me and I promise to slap that top rocker on your cut."

"I'm patching in?" I ask in shock. "Seriously? It's finally gonna happen?"

"It's happening, kid. First, get my sister away from this fucking hurricane," he assures me.

"I'm on it. I'll leave right now," I say before I end the call.

Fuck, this job is one of my easiest since I start prospecting. Picking up some chick and driving her a few hours inland is nothing compared to disposing of dead bodies.

Oh yeah, I've done that for my patch.

Hell, I would do anything to finally get patched into the Savage Kings MC. It's the only connection to my father I'll ever have, and since I left home, well, it's the only social life I have now, period.

...

AN HOUR LATER, I'm standing outside the locked apartments, in the pouring rain that's blowing sideways, hitting me right in the face, waiting for someone to come in or out of the fucking door.

The whole campus looks like a wasteland. They've placed sandbags all around the edges of the brick buildings, but the water is already halfway up them, covering the tops of my steel toe boots. Thanks to the whipping wind, an occasional piece of trash swirls around me. When I'm finally able to locate the right call button on the intercom for Apartment two-twenty-eight B, I hit it but get no response.

Finally, a chick comes running out of the building with a raincoat over her head and arms full of bags. She's in too big of a rush to see me, or care when I slip through the door before it shuts. I take a second to relish the dry environment before I push my wet hair out of my eyes and trudge up the first set of stairs I come to. My soggy boots squeak and echo on the linoleum the entire way. The only other sound in the building is the faint hum of electricity from the fluorescent lights. "Two-twenty-eight B, Two-twenty-eight B," I repeat over and over again once I'm on the second floor. Finally, I find the right apartment and raise my knuckles to knock.

Not a minute later, the door cracks open just an inch, revealing one-half of a pale, petite face, her single dark chocolate eye wide in terror...and a yellow kitten climbing up her shoulder.

"Can I help you?" she asks, looking me up and down while trying to keep the cat from escaping.

I'm one hundred percent certain there's no fucking way this girl could be War's sister. The dude is enormous and she's...tiny, like no bigger than one of his tree trunk thighs.

"Yeah, I'm looking for Aubrey," I say, then pause when that

doesn't sound exactly right. "No, shit, it's Audrey, I think. Audrey O'Neil."

"You sure about that?" the girl asks me after I stammer over the name.

"Yeah. Yes. Definitely Audrey. Maybe?"

"Well, I don't know who you are, so I can't give you information about...my roommate." She hesitates, like she was going to say her friend or something else, but maybe they don't get along or whatever.

"Come on. I really need to find her, and the eye of the hurricane is coming up on the city fast!"

"How do you know Audrey?" she questions me.

"I don't know her," I respond. "Her brother War sent me."

"You're friends with her brother?" Her eye lowers to look at my leather cut in disbelief.

"Sort of, yeah. I guess you could say that."

"Prove it."

"What?" I ask in confusion.

Removing the kitten's claws from her shoulder, she readjusts her hold on it and says, "Prove that you're actually a friend of Audrey's brother, and maybe I'll tell you where you can find her."

"Okay, um..." Thinking fast, I point to the flash on the front of my wet leather cut, the ones that say, "Savage Kings MC" and "Emerald Isle" underneath. "War is a member of the Savage Kings and I'm prospecting for them."

"What's the Savage Kings?" she asks.

"It's, ah, it's a motorcycle club. Hasn't Aubrey told you about all that?"

"*Audrey*," she corrects, when I get the name wrong again. "And no, she's never mentioned anything about her brother being in a motorcycle club. What else you got?"

Fuck, this chick is being difficult.

I pull out my burner phone from the inner pocket of my cut to call War, but it's powered down with a black screen. The damn thing is dead, and I left in such a hurry I forgot the fucking charger. "Shit.

My phone is dead, or I would call and let you talk to her brother. Can you just please tell me where Audrey is? I'm supposed to pick her up and get her out of town before the storm gets any closer."

"No."

"No?" I repeat.

"You don't look very trustworthy, so you need to turn around and leave." Now her gaze is lowered to the tattoos on my forearms, like they're some type of heathen label.

"What? This is just a little ink. I'm totally trustworthy," I tell her. "All I want to know is if Audrey is here or not, and if not, where I can find her," I say, trying to look around her into the apartment.

"You need to leave before I call campus security," the girl threatens.

"Good luck with that," I reply, thinking about the roads on the way in. "There's nobody on campus."

"Guess we'll see," she counters.

Fuck, I'm really starting to lose my patience, and I'm not letting her call the rent-a-cops on me. I need to see if Audrey is in the apartment and if not, make this girl cough up the information, so we can get the hell out of dodge.

When a sudden, loud crash of thunder distracts her, I throw my shoulder into the door, causing the girl to stumble back enough for me to squeeze inside.

"Hey! Get out of here!" she says before she lowers the kitten to the ground to come at me. The cat scurries away further into the apartment while she presses her small palms to my chest and bicep, to try and force me back out. Her attempt is futile since I may not be a huge guy, but I'm a helluva lot bigger than her by at least a foot and probably seventy or eight pounds. Thanks to Reece's training last year, I'm also a helluva lot tougher than I was a few years back.

I grab her narrow wrists in each of my hands and then spin her around, so her back is against the door that slams shut while I hold her hands above her head.

"Audrey?" I yell out. "Audrey, are you here?"

12

There's no response.

"Okay, enough of the runaround," I narrow my eyes and tell the girl I have pinned to the door. Her long, flowing dark hair is thick and wavy, hanging down to her waist, the strands almost the same color as her big chocolate eyes that are currently glaring up at me. "Tell me where the fuck Audrey is right now!"

The tiny girl scoffs indignantly at my "tough guy" approach. Guess it needs a little more practice. "Or what? You'll hurt me?"

"No," I huff, as I try to figure out some way to make her talk. I would never hurt a woman, especially not War's sister's roommate.

"Tell me or I'll..."

"You'll what?" she asks, defiance filling her brown eyes.

"I'll..." Shit, what am I gonna do to make her talk?

Finally, I decide to threaten her with the only thing that comes to mind, since I wouldn't physically hurt her.

Thinking fast, I transfer both of her wrists into one of my much bigger hands, then I lower my other hand to grasp her side. I couldn't see what she had on through the crack in the door, but now I get an up-close look at her soft purple pajama pants and short-sleeve top that's decorated with seashells and...lace lining the edges of the plunging V-neck. It hits me that she looks like a girl who is planning on settling in for a long Netflix binge instead of evacuating, like everyone else on the entire East Coast.

Strange decision, but she's not my responsibility.

"Tell me, or I'll tickle it out of you."

"Tickle me?" she repeats. "That'll never work. I'm not ticklish."

I barely even flex my fingers, and she starts squirming against the door and laughing. Since the front of my body was almost pressed to hers to begin with, all the wiggling has her stomach rubbing against the crotch of my jeans. That's the moment my cock goes from strictly professional to *well, what do we have here.*

In his defense, it doesn't take much for him to get excited. He's been waiting twenty-one long years to sink inside of a woman and he's starting to get rather impatient about my status as a virgin.

It's not like I haven't had plenty of opportunities at the clubhouse, or a blowjob before, but the night Cynthia was cozying up to me about a year ago is the first time I've ever seen my own death reflecting back in someone else's eyes. Reece's, to be specific. I know he's a dangerous son of a bitch who could easily rip me in half. From then on, it seemed like a good idea to steer clear of the club girls to avoid accidentally pissing off one of the members.

Now is not the time or place to be thinking with my dick either. I need to find War's sister and get us the hell out of town before the storm closes in. It's already raining cats and dogs out there.

"Tell me where she is," I demand as my fingers continue to tickle the girl's side, while trying to tell my cock to behave.

"Okay, okay!" she says over her laughter, so I finally relent, even though I don't take my hands off of her just yet.

CHAPTER TWO

Audrey O'Neil

THERE'S NO WAY IN HELL I'M LEAVING THE COMFORT AND safety of my apartment while the worst storm in history rages around us outside.

I'm angry at my brother for not coming to get me sooner before the weather got bad, and then sending some...some random guy to haul me out when he knows how shaky and freaked out I get during thunder and lightning.

I was never a fan of storms *before* the one that killed my parents. Now...well, now I can't help but think that one of these days, god is planning to take me out the same way. I'm only twenty-two. I'm not ready to die!

And if I don't come up with something to keep this guy busy, he's gonna try to drag me outside when I'm obviously safer here.

Despite how handsome and sexy he is in his bad boy leather with his full kissable lips, I'm not leaving with him.

"So, where is Audrey?" he asks, when I take too long to answer.

LANE HART & D.B. WEST

"She's already gone," I reply.

"Gone? Gone where?" he snaps, his hand tightening on my side in a not entirely uncomfortable way.

"She left, so what does it matter?" I lie.

"When? When did she leave?" he asks with his brow furrowed.

"This morning, on a, ah, university bus headed to Asheville."

"Bullshit!" he says, his face still only inches away from mine. "Her brother wouldn't have told me to come get her unless he knew she was still here!"

"Sorry, but she's long gone," I tell him with a shrug.

"Give me her number. Or call her and find out exactly where she is right now, so that I can follow her."

"No," I refuse. Using a phone during a lightning storm is like begging god to strike you down. I don't want to be in the same apartment when that shit goes down.

"I need to use your phone! Mine's dead. At least let me call War," he begs.

"No."

This time, his jaw falls open almost comically before he recovers and says, "You're awfully little to be such a big pain in my ass!"

"You're not supposed to use the phone during a storm," I point out.

"Why not? Especially when it's an emergency. And this, well, this is a fucking emergency!" He still hasn't let my hands go, and now we're so close, you couldn't slip a piece of paper between us. "Only corded phones are dangerous in storms, not cell phones. And there's a hurricane coming! If I don't find this girl soon, everything I've worked for will be for nothing!"

"What have you worked for?" I ask.

"My patch."

"A patch?"

"Getting the patches on the back of my cut that make me a member of the Savage Kings," he explains.

16

"So, you're not a member right now?"

"No."

"But Warren...Audrey's brother is?" I inquire.

"Yes! He's the one who can make or break my membership!"

"So, you're saying that he has a lot of power in this motorcycle club?" I ask, since this is all news to me. I would think the guy is lying except, what reason would he have to do that? Warren must have been keeping this shit from me.

"Yes, War's the Sergeant-at-Arms to the president."

"What does the Sergeant of Arms do?"

"Jeez, you ask a lot of questions," he grumbles. When I stare blankly at him in expectation, he finally sighs and says, "Fine, this is nothing you can't search on the internet. The Sergeant-at-Arms is the one who is always packing heat. It's his job to protect the president."

"When you say 'packing heat,' you mean...carry a *gun*?"

"Yes," he replies on an exasperated sigh.

None of this is sounding anything like my straight-laced, Army vet brother. He's never hurt a soul! Even when he was in the military, he was just a mechanic, not the guy with a gun. Warren is kind and he takes care of people, especially me and Ren.

But if what this guy is saying is true, then maybe I don't know the real Warren at all.

There must be a good reason why the state took my nephew Ren from him just a few weeks ago and refuses to give him back. And it can't all be just because Marcie screwed up.

How long has Warren been lying to me? And what else do I not know about the man who raised me?

"Does he...does he like, kill people?" I ask in shock. "He doesn't do that, does he?"

"What? I can't tell you that," he huffs. "And I'm not going to answer any more of your fucking questions. Either you can tell me where your phone is, or I'll tear this place apart looking for it."

"You'll never find it unless I tell you where it is," I assure him, since it's turned off and stuffed under my mattress. I take lightning *very* seriously.

Blowing out another frustrated minty breath that flutters over my face, he looks me right in the eye and flexes his fingers that are still clutching my side. "Am I gonna have to tickle you again?"

Lightning shoots across the sky, making the room flicker with a bluish tint right before a booming crack of thunder strikes so loudly in the silence that I let out a shriek. I swear I hear the windows in the apartment rattle from the intensity.

The guy holding me hostage looks over his shoulder at the apartment behind him, then turns back to me with his brow furrowed. "Why is all your furniture shoved against the windows?" he asks.

"Ah, well, it's just nice to have an extra layer of protection between the windows and the storm."

"Uh-huh," he mutters, like he thinks I'm crazy. To most normal people, I probably am a little insane.

But they've never had their worst fear take the lives of both of their parents.

"Why haven't you left town yet?" the guy asks. "Why didn't you leave with Audrey?"

"Because I didn't want to," I answer.

"When the governor says you need to evacuate, you should probably listen," he argues.

"No."

"So, you're just gonna stay here, *alone*, during the worst hurricane ever to hit the coast?" he asks. I have to swallow past the panic climbing up my throat before I can answer.

"Yes."

"What about your parents? They must be worried sick," he says.

"My parents are dead."

"Shit, that sucks," he says in a rush. And instead of apologizing for something that wasn't even in his control to begin with like most people, he says, "My dad's dead too. I never even got to meet him."

"Seriously?" I ask in surprise.

"Yeah," he replies, then huffs out a laugh. "I didn't even find out who he was until a few years ago. By then, my mom told me he was already dead."

"That sucks," I tell him, repeating his own words.

"Yeah, it does. But I was able to find out who he was. He built the entire Savage Kings MC and was their president before he died of cancer."

"So that's why it means so much for you to get your patch?" I guess.

"Yeah," he says on an exhale before he realizes I've tried to change the subject. "Now that we've bonded over our mutual parental loss, how about you do me a solid and give me your phone?"

Dammit. Now he had to go and put a guilt trip on me.

I don't want him to get in trouble with my brother. At the same time, though, I'm pissed at Warren, and I'm not going to leave the comfort of my safe and dry apartment either.

But this guy is persistent. Eventually, he may even find my phone. When he talks to my brother, he'll know who I am and then I wouldn't put it past him to throw me over his shoulder and haul me out of here if Warren says to do it. He seems very dedicated to the leather jacket gods and his long-lost father.

If I've learned anything during my three years of college, it's that there's one thing that always works on men to get what I want. Besides, this guy is incredibly hot, and my inhibitions are low, thanks to the Xanax I've been popping like Tic Tacs ever since the weatherman first said the word "hurricane" a few days ago.

All I need is to postpone him a little longer, and then it'll be too bad outside to leave, even if I wanted to. That's not something I'm looking forward to either, but we're on the second floor of my building where the water can't reach us. As long as the windows hold, we'll be just fine for a few days.

So, I look him right in his gray eyes and say, "Fuck me, and the phone is all yours."

The handsome stranger stares down at me, unblinking, like he's trying to figure out if I'm joking or not.

"You can't be serious," he eventually says, still holding my wrists above my head while his big, hard body presses me into the door just a tiny bit harder.

"What's your name?" I ask him, blowing a strand of my dark hair out of my eyes.

"Maddox."

"Well, Maddox, the storm is getting worse, so unless you're going to go out into it to find another phone, you better hurry."

"Hurry, and...fuck you?" he reiterates.

"That's right," I tell him. "Haven't you noticed? This is an all-girl university. You're the first guy my age that I've seen in a very long time."

"Are you screwing with me?" he asks.

"Nope."

"Are you...are you a virgin?" he asks. I'm not sure if his voice sounded hopeful or wary.

"No." Despite my innocent little girl appearance, I've been with three men.

"No?" he repeats.

"I traded my virginity to my Physics professor last year."

"You're kidding," Maddox says.

"Well, it was more than once. I was failing, so it took a few times before I finally got a C, then the C turned into a B, then the B to an A. Eventually, it was just extra credit and I made it to the top of my class."

"You were sleeping with your professor to improve your grades."

Nodding, I continue to tell him something that no one else knows about me. "Professor Burrows would lock the auditorium doors after class was over, and then fuck me right there on his desk."

"That's pretty hardcore and...kind of hot," Maddox says, his eyes lowering to my lips.

"So, what's it gonna be?" I ask. "Clock's ticking."

"Why do you want me? We just met, and I-I don't even know your name."

"Does any of that really matter to you?" I question, knowing by the tenting in his jeans that the answer is no.

CHAPTER THREE

Maddox

"DOES ANY OF THAT REALLY MATTER TO YOU?"

Her response is echoing around in my head, yet for some reason, I can no longer remember the question I asked.

It's absolutely horrible timing, I know, but all the blood in my head is accumulating in my dick that's now so swollen that it's throbbing in time with my racing heartbeat.

And what other choice do I have here? I need to use her phone. Sure, there are other phones in the world, but I'm here and she's so warm and close to me. I mean, her phone is close. It seems like my virginity is a small price to pay to be with the tiny seductress in exchange for a few calls on her cell, which could mean getting my patch or losing it all.

Honestly, I don't even know why I've waited this long to have sex. There were no women in military school. Then, even though I was horny as shit, I didn't actually want my first time to be with a club slut who could blink and forget it ever happened.

I may not know this girl's name, but she's beautiful and she's making me an offer I couldn't refuse even if I tried.

"We'll have to make this fast," I warn her. I'm sure I won't be able to last long, even if I wasn't in a hurry and needed to find War's sister. At least she's out of town and safe in the mountains by now. I just need to let War know she was gone before I got here. I'm sure he'll understand...

"If it's going to be fast, then you better get me ready," she replies.

"Get you ready?" I repeat in confusion.

"I want it to be good for me too," she says, and understanding finally dawns. She wants me to finger her or to go down on her—maybe both—first. The thought of doing either has my eyes glassing over, making the apartment blurry with a hazy lust. If I get any more turned on, I may very well go blind.

"Right, yeah, I want it to be good for you too," I tell her, even though the only sexual experience I have is sneaking off to my room to dry hump a girl in my bed once. I was fourteen and my parents were home, but busy entertaining their dinner guests. That was when I went to school with girls too, before they shipped me off to the military academy.

I'll be damned if I tell this girl all of that, though.

Fake it until you make her come is my new motto.

I still have her pinned to the apartment door at my mercy, and she basically just gave me a green light to do anything I want to her.

Fuck, where do I even start? I mean, I've watched porn but I'm guessing that the down and dirty fucking isn't what real women want.

Kissing.

I should probably start by kissing her, right?

I don't ask her that but instead lower my lips to hers to give it a try. She moans, and I feel her body go limp in my grip. Her pinned wrists lower a few inches and her stomach, where my thumb is pressed into, dips with her gasping breath. Since her lips are already parted, I slip my tongue in to touch hers, and...thunder crashes.

The world shakes under my boots.

It's fucking amazing.

And there's a chance it could also be the storm outside, but I'm pretty sure it's her.

Us.

While our kiss deepens, my left hand slides under her pajama top, and then it's cupping her heavy, braless tit, my thumb strumming her beaded nipple. She's so soft and smooth and...perfect.

Damn, I wish my other hand was available to get to her other breast. But I'm afraid that if I let *her* hands go, she'll touch me and then this will be over before it gets started. I have to keep my hips back for the same reason, unable to endure her grinding against the bulge in the front of my jeans.

"Lower," she whispers against my lips. And even though I know exactly what and where she's referring to, I move my hand down her side and then give the elastic of her pajama bottoms a tug.

"You want me to get rid of these for you?" I ask.

"Uh-huh," she agrees with a puff of air against my mouth and a vigorous nod, so I yank them down so hard, they puddle around her feet.

I have to break our kiss then because I need to get a look at her in her panties before I rip them off too.

She's wearing a miniscule pair made out of pale pink satin. It's not a thong but it's just as sexy. And fuck, I need to touch her.

Unsure where to start, I run my knuckle from the top of the waistband down the silky material covering her mound until I get to the hot, wet spot in the center.

When she squirms against the door in response, I tell her, "Looks like I found another place where you're ticklish."

"Keep going," she gasps, eyes heavy-lidded when she looks up at me.

There's no way I'll be the one to put a stop to this.

She's offering herself up to me, a starving man, like she's an all-you-can-eat buffet of naughty temptation.

Since I want to see her in nothing but the panties, I yank her pajama top up, pulling her head through it and leaving the material on her arms that are still raised and trapped above her head. Then I take a step back while keeping my grip on her wrists to take in every delicious inch.

Fuck, she's perfect. All-natural tits big enough to jiggle, but not so big and overwhelming that I can't handle them, and a lean narrow waist before a swell of hips right where the dainty panties cover the best part. Leaning down, I capture the nipple I haven't touched yet in my mouth. I give it a suck before ravishing it with my tongue. Switching to place a few kisses on the other breast, I glance down to watch my big, calloused hand disappear down the front of her feminine little panties. It's an obscene sight—like I'm too rough-neck to be touching such a petite, innocent woman in such a vulgar way.

"God, yes," she gasps when my fingertips reach the top of her slit.

"Lower?" I ask.

"Yes."

She's so wet my middle finger sinks right inside of her slick pussy.

Another crack of thunder sounds behind me at the same time, making her body clamp down on my finger and reminding me there's a hurricane coming. I'm supposed to be doing something important.

Fuck if I remember what it was right this second, standing in this apartment, with a beautiful woman letting me get inside of her pink panties.

Letting her nipple slip from my mouth, I ask, "You okay?"

"Uh-huh. Don't stop," she tells me.

I slant my mouth over hers to start kissing her again, and my eyes fall shut as her body relaxes, allowing my finger to sink deep inside of her before I start pumping it in and out. Her hips swivel, and she moans against my lips as I get her good and ready to take my cock. It's a big one, if I do say so myself. And right now, it doesn't really seem possible that it'll all fit inside of someone so small.

26

My eyes pop open when there's another flash of lightning, immediately followed by a rumble of thunder.

"Shit, that was close," I grumble.

"Yeah," she agrees. "Take me to my bedroom."

Yes! A bed is exactly what we need to get this done.

Without further instructions, I release her wrists, letting them
lower as I scoop her up by both ass cheeks and turn around to find a
fucking bed. And it needs to be soon because now those damp
panties and all that lies underneath are pressed against my aching
cock that's trapped behind my zipper.

"This one," she directs me to the first room on the left. There's an
overhead light on, showing a nice room with a high ceiling, photos of
dolphins and sea turtles on the walls...with two tall dressers in front
of the windows. It looks strange as shit but before I can ask about it, I
spot the perfectly made bed done up in what other color but more
ultra girly pink.

There could be dancing unicorns on it for all I care. It's our final
destination, the spot where I'm finally going to lose my virginity.
Thank fuck. I was almost as worried about losing it before getting
patched in as a Savage King as I am *about* getting patched in. The
Kings are badasses, not pussy virgins, that's for sure.

I lower her to the bed and follow her down, groaning when our
bodies line right up in the way God intended.

She rolls her hips to rub herself against the bulge running down
the thigh of my jeans, while at the same time, her hands push my cut
down my shoulders. I draw back from her and kneel between her
legs, removing my cut and then peeling my T-shirt over my head as
her hands fumble with my belt buckle. Before I can stand up to finish
getting undressed, she pops the button on my jeans and lowers the
zipper, then shoves my pants and boxers down my thighs. When my
cock finally springs free, she leans forward and grabs the base of it,
leaning forward and giving the tip a gentle lick.

"Jesus," she whispers, reaching up to run her free hand down my
abs. She uses one fingernail to trace the muscles on my stomach

before taking a deep, steadying breath and lowering her head to lick the underside of my cock, letting her tongue linger over every inch as she makes her way back up to the head. Wrapping her lips around the crown, she swirls her tongue around, sending a jolt of such intense pleasure through me that I feel my balls tighten. There's no way in hell I'm going to embarrass myself by blowing a surprise load in her mouth when we're just getting started, so I reach down to grab her breast, then bend down to her, pulling my cock away as I kiss her and force her back down to the mattress.

"I want to try to suck it," she gasps as I begin kissing my way down her neck.

"You'll get plenty of chances," I growl in reply. She gasps and laughs as my tongue finds the spot on her side I had tickled earlier, and she grabs my head as she tries to roll away.

When she pushes my head, I dive lower, my chin pushing down the waistband of her dainty pink panties as I press my lips and tongue into the dark, neatly-trimmed patch of hair on her mound. I grab her hips and rise up just enough to drag her panties down her legs. While I have her knees raised, I press my face into her, licking each of her lower lips before forcing my tongue deeper into her.

Her legs tremble as she reaches up to dispose of her panties, then she collapses back onto her pillows. She gasps and moans as my lips find her clit. I trap it and suck on it, lashing at it with my tongue. She grabs the comforter in both fists as my mouth becomes frantic on her pussy, her bucking hips spurring me on until her thighs clamp together and her stomach clenches under my hand.

"Fuck, fuck, fuck!" she screeches as she slams her pussy into my face, the orgasm that rips through her seeming to last forever as my jaw begins to ache from the relentless tongue-lashing I'm giving her. Once she finally collapses back onto the comforter and her thighs fall open, I rest my chin on her mound and eye her warily. I'm not entirely sure if what just happened was a good thing.

"You okay up there?" I snort.

"Getting better," she gasps, her breasts trembling with her rapid breaths. She reaches down to give my hair a gentle tug, and I stand up to finish stripping off my pants. "Do you have a condom?"

I nod and manage to dig out my wallet, where the single condom I've kept for "emergencies" is stored. It looks a little worse for wear, but I toss it on the bed while I struggle to get the rest of my clothes off. Tearing the condom open, she looks me up and down as I stand beside her bed.

"God, I hope these are big enough." She laughs as she reaches over to grab my throbbing cock and force the rubber down my length. When it's fully unrolled, she pauses, staring at my cock in her hand with a blank expression I can't read.

"What's wrong?" I ask her as I kneel on the bed, leaning in to kiss her and lead her back down to the mattress.

"Nothing, I was just thinking I've never run out of condom before." She grins, reaching down between us and lining up our bodies. Once she guides me to her opening, she grabs my hips, eagerly pulling me toward her.

I resist only for a moment, confused by what she said. "You've never run out of condoms?" I try to clarify.

"No, I've never run out of *condom*," she laughs. "You've got too much cock for this brand. I've never seen one unroll all the way before and still have skin left. Now quit talking," she demands as she leans up to kiss me, while still pulling at my hips.

I give myself over to the moment, kissing her fiercely as I let her guide me forward. She sets the pace with her hands on my hips, pulling me to her and almost slamming her pussy onto me, before a trembling gasp breaks free from her lips as she pauses, wiggling her hips as if struggling to pack more of me inside.

"Take your time," I whisper into her ear as I cradle her head in one hand, the other covering her hip. I hope she takes the hint, as the combination of this woman's incredibly sexy body, words, and motions is almost too much for me to withstand. The pressure in my lower belly is unbelievable, like nothing I have ever felt in my life.

Instead of responding, she bites her lip, locking eyes with me before she wraps her heels behind my thighs. She entwines her arms around my back, and then with a cry that could be either pleasure or pain, she squeezes me to her until the base of my cock grinds against her and my balls slap her ass. She throws her head back, gasping as she bucks her hips against me, so I wrap my arms around her arched back and try to hold on as she rides me from below.

A few moments later, she stills in my arms, and after giving me a long, deep kiss, she says, "I can't believe I came like that. I'm okay now, I think I'm used to it. You can move, but go easy at first, all right?"

If I had any experience with sex at all, I would have recognized that she was having another orgasm.

I give her a nod, so overwhelmed by the entire experience, I can't even speak. The way she moves, she feels, she sounds, it's all too much. I take a deep shuddering breath as I start to gently rock my hips, her moaning and the trembling in her thighs and pussy quickly pushing me to the brink.

"You're so fucking good, I can't..." I gasp.

"Oh god, I'm coming again!" she cries as her nails dig into my back. I take that as my cue and quicken my pace, the pressure and need so great that I completely lose myself. Our lips crash together in a frenzied kiss as I pour into her, our cries mixing together as we climax.

I'm still coming hard when suddenly everything goes dark. That's never happened before when I was jerking off or getting a blowjob. Must be just how good her pussy feels.

As I start to catch my breath, I realize the room is still really dark.

"Did the lights go out or did you fuck me so good I went blind?" I ask her.

"Power's out."

"Shit," I mutter as I scramble off of her and start getting dressed. "This was fun and all," I say, in the understatement of the year, as I pull my jeans up my legs, "but I need your phone right fucking now so that I can find Aubrey."

"Okay, but it's *Audrey*," she replies as she rolls to her side. Propping her head up on her bent elbow, she watches me dress. "And don't stand within five feet of me while you're using it."

I pull my shirt over my head and ask, "Fine. Where's your phone?"

"Very close. You won't believe just how close it is."

"Just tell me already!" I exclaim as I sit down on the side of the bed to put my soaked socks and shoes back on in the dark.

Slipping her hand under the mattress, she pulls out the thin phone and hands it to me.

"Fuck," I mutter as I take it and power it on, making the screen brighten up the room. "I don't know if I can remember War's number."

"He's in my contacts," she says.

"What now?" I ask. Did she say War's number is saved in her contacts? Pulling up the list of friends and family, it's so short that I quickly get to the W's. I tap on Warren's name to call him. While it's ringing at my ear, I ask her, "Why do you have War's number in *your* phone?"

"Because he's *my* brother."

I freeze as her words start to sink in slowly.

"Audrey! Are you okay? I'm so damn sorry I couldn't get down there. You wouldn't believe the shitstorm we've been through," War says when he answers the phone, thinking I'm her and confirming what I was beginning to fear.

Unable to come up with any words other than *oh shit*, I thrust the phone into Audrey's face.

Audrey! She's fucking Audrey!

"Hi, Warren," she says sweetly, apparently forgetting her "five foot" rule. "Where are you? Yeah, he did. His phone died and mine has been off." Audrey looks up at me, her angelic face glowing, thanks to the phone at her ear. "We just got to Raleigh," she lies, and then has the nerve to wink at me as she digs my grave deeper.

No, no, no. This cannot be happening!

31

I fucked War's sister and now she's lying to him, so *I'll* have to lie to him. I'm so damn screwed!

"I don't think we can make it to Greensboro," Audrey tells her brother. "In case you haven't heard, there's a gas shortage, thanks to everyone draining the stations! Yes, I'm fine. We'll be fine," she assures him.

We are *not* fucking fine.

I'm the furthest thing you can get from fine!

Everything I've worked for with the MC is circling the goddamn drain all because I was a horny idiot. Why couldn't Audrey have been a two-hundred-pound female bodybuilder with golden eyes? If she looked like War in a wig, I *never* would've made this mistake. Instead, she looks nothing at all like him. There's zero resemblance!

She must have been adopted, that's all there is to it.

"We need to get off the phone, Warren! Yes, and I love you too," Audrey says softly into the phone before she holds it up to me, causing her bare tits to jiggle distractingly. I have to clench my fists to keep from lowering a hand to grab one. "He wants to talk to you now."

F.M.L.

Swallowing hard around the knot in my throat, I un-ball my fist to take the device and try to make my voice steady when I say, "Yes, sir?"

"How bad has she been?" he asks.

So fucking bad, I start to say.

But no, that has to be a trick question.

"Ah, I'm not sure what you mean," I respond instead, while scratching the back of my head with my free hand.

"Her astraphobia," War clarifies, as if I have any fucking idea what that word means.

"Her *what*?" I ask. Hearing this, Audrey grabs a pillow and covers her face with it.

"Audrey has a severe fear of thunderstorms, but she sounded

32

pretty calm. You must have got her inland before the weather got bad."

Glancing over at the heavy furniture blocking the windows, that, along with the spontaneous seduction, starts to finally make sense. Guess the orgasms I gave her were also calming...

"Maddox? You there?" War asks when I remain lost in my thoughts for too long.

Finally, I'm able to say, "Oh, yeah, Audrey's fine. I mean, she seems to be doing okay."

"You're going to hunker down in Raleigh to wait out the hurricane?" he asks. And since the sexy liar has now backed me into a corner, I have no choice but to go along with the fib.

"Yep. We'll stay here in Raleigh until it's safe to go back," I say. "Everything is completely under control."

And it will be. Because as soon as I hang up the phone, you can bet your ass that I'll be dragging his sister downstairs, throwing her in the van, and taking her to fucking Raleigh. "How are things going there?" I ask War to spin the conversation back to him.

"It's been one helluva day," War grumbles before lowering his voice. "But that's a long story for another time. I don't want Audrey to know how bad it was just yet."

"Understood," I reply, knowing it must have been serious if he asked me to come get his sister instead of doing it himself.

"I appreciate you picking Audrey up for me and keeping her safe," he says.

"No problem," I tell him, even though I know he's not finished.

"Do I need to go through the formalities of warning you not to touch my little sister while you're watching out for her?"

"No, sir, absolutely not," I respond, squeezing my eyes shut as I recall looking at and touching every amazing inch of her, inside and out.

"Because you know what would happen if you step a toe out of line, don't you?" he threatens.

"I do," I agree.

"The beating you would get after I take your cut would make Holden's beatdown look like a cat fight," War elaborates, reminding me of the day every one of the Savage Kings got to pound their fists into the prospect who turned out to be a rat.

"Yes, sir. I understand."

"Good. Take care and we'll talk soon," he says before hanging up on me.

"Why didn't you tell me?" I snap at Audrey when I toss her phone down next to her. She bats it away so that it hits the floor instead. Before she even has a chance to respond, I'm pacing at the foot of her bed, running my fingers through my hair. "Oh god. I'm so dead. War is going to kill me! How could you do this to me?"

"Are you really mad at me for fucking you so good you thought I made you blind?" she asks. "I didn't hear any complaints during—"

"I lost my virginity just to use your phone and get this job done!" I exclaim. "And now I'm gonna die because of the one goddamn time I caved and had sex with a woman!"

"Whoa!" Audrey sits up on the edge of the mattress without bothering to cover up any of her nakedness and says, "You were a *virgin*? Are you joking right now?" Blinking at me when I refuse to say it again, she tells me, "Dude, if you had walked onto this campus any other day when it wasn't being evacuated, your virginity wouldn't have lasted five seconds."

"Oh yeah? You don't think so?" I ask. "Because there are plenty of club sluts who tried to fuck me, and I turned all of them down."

"Club sluts?"

"Never mind, forget it," I grumble. "Just get up and get dressed. As soon as you pack a bag we're leaving."

"No, we're not," she counters.

"Oh, yes we fucking are!" I shout. "I *have* to get you to Raleigh now. And you better pray that there's not a gas shortage or my head is gonna get knocked off by your brother, and it'll be all your fault!"

"So, you're saying that you wouldn't have fucked me if I had told you who I was?" she asks coyly.

"Of course not!" I yell. "Why? Why did you lie?"

"Because I'm not leaving this apartment with you or anyone else!" she shrieks as she gets to her feet and stands a foot away from me...still completely naked.

Do you know how hard it is for a horny twenty-one-year old to argue with a naked woman? It's nearly impossible, because now I'm thinking about being inside of her again and I have no clue what we were fighting about.

Shutting my eyes helps, even though the image of her tiny curvy body still lingers until I think of carburetors and brake pads. There! Now, what were we arguing about? Oh, right.

"Get some clothes on so we can go!" I tell her.

"Why are you yelling at me with your eyes closed?" she asks.

"Because you're naked!"

"And I'm going to stay this way. I don't go out in storms. Ever!"

When my eyes twitch, trying to pop open and get another look at her, I slap my palm over them and say, "If War had showed up to get you, I'm guessing you would've been dressed and he would've thrown you over his shoulder and carried you out if he needed to."

"I would've convinced him to stay too."

"How?" I ask.

"I would tell him we should stay because I don't want us to end up like our mom and dad who died in agony, trapped in their car after they hit a tree."

Lowering my palm from my face, I ask, "That's what happened to them?"

"Yes," she answers, crossing her arms over her bare chest.

"War never said..."

"If they had just stayed home that night instead of going out in that shitty storm, they would still be alive!"

"I'm sorry," I tell her softly, understanding her fear much more clearly now that I know her past. "We'll stay here."

"Really?" she asks, her big chocolate eyes wide and hopeful. The fact that what little natural light there is in the room makes her unshed tears glisten is just the final touch for making me completely cave. "You won't drag me out into the hurricane?"

"Not if you won't ever tell your brother that we slept together or that we never made it to Raleigh."

"Deal," she agrees. Uncrossing her arms, she holds out her palm to me.

When I accept her handshake, she cheerfully says, "Hi, I'm Audrey. Audrey O'Neil. Warren's sister," while our palms are still clasped.

Grinning despite how fucked I am, I tell her, "It's nice to meet you, Audrey. I'm Maddox and I'm already a huge fan of your...lack of clothing."

"Why don't you take yours back off and get comfortable?" she suggests, letting my hand go to take a step forward and get to work undoing my pants again. "It looks like we may be here for a while together without any power. Any ideas for what we can do to entertain ourselves?"

"A few." When her palm lowers to cup me through the denim, I can't help but groan with need.

"If you were a virgin, then you have a lot of catching up to do in bed."

Nodding, I tell her, "That sounds amazing, but I used my only condom earlier..."

"Shit," Audrey mutters.

"You don't have any?" I guess, my entire body deflating in disappointment. I mean, yeah, there are some things we could do without rubbers, but I *really* want to do more of the stuff with them.

"No. But maybe my roommate does."

When she starts to walk past me toward the door, I put a hand on her arm to stop her. "I'm probably the stupidest man ever to say this, but would you mind putting some clothes on? I'm afraid that if you don't, I'll say to hell with protection, throw you down, and fuck you again anyways."

Audrey reaches for the bottom hem of my T-shirt and then lifts it up and over my head. Before I can blink, she's putting it on and covering up her luscious body.

"That better?" she asks. I'm not sure which is sexier, her naked or her wearing nothing but my white tee. It's so transparent, I can see her nipples through it, and short enough that if I turned her around, I'm pretty sure her ass cheeks would be hanging out. Okay, I have to see for myself. Grasping her shoulders, I spin her around and then curse when I find out I was right. Seeing her bare bottom teasing me in such a way makes me want to bend her over the bed and slam inside of her so bad that the room spins before I get control of myself.

So, the good news is that at least when War kills me, I will no longer be an inexperienced virgin.

CHAPTER FOUR

Audrey

MADDOX AND I STRIKE GOLD IN MY ROOMMATES' NIGHTSTAND, specifically a family-size box of gold-foil Magnum condoms. The rest of our first day together passes in a blur, as he and I stretch our imaginations to their sexual limits. Now that he's popped his cherry, he seems completely addicted, and for my part, I've never had such a fine "tool" to work with in the bedroom.

It's just after sunset when I collapse on Maddox's chest, completely spent from riding him for the last half hour. As we both struggle to catch our breath, I inhale deeply and crinkle my nose at our acrid smell. "Is that me or you?" I ask him.

"I think it's both of us." He laughs, sniffing at my neck. "Smells like sweat, cum, and latex in here."

"Yuck." I grimace and stick my tongue out at him. "The water should still run for a while, even with the power out. Let's see if we can get a quick shower together."

"Oh shit, the thought of soaping up your tits and taking you in the shower..." Maddox's naughty thought trails off, but his cock, still wedged deep inside me, gives an agreeable throb as if to finish his sentence.

"Come on, stinky," I urge him, as I finally dismount and stand by the side of the bed, stretching. I pick up the flashlight I left on the nightstand and lead Maddox down the hall to the bathroom. While I turn on the shower, he throws the condom away in the trash, then comes up behind me to rub himself against my backside.

"This may not go quite the way we wanted," I say as I pull my hand out of the shower. I flick a handful of cold water on him, giggling as he jerks away from me.

"Holy shit, that's freezing! There's no hot water, huh?" he asks as he leans past me to test it himself.

"Doesn't look like it. Let's make this quick, then we can towel each other off and have some fun!"

We jump into the shower together, but rather than fighting over who gets to stand under the water, we both struggle to stay out of the freezing spray. We soap up quickly, rinse each other down with a variety of squeals and curses, then jump back out together.

"Are you sure you don't want to get out of here?" Maddox asks me as he stands on the shower mat, dripping and shivering. "That was awful!"

I'm too cold to even respond, so I throw him a towel and use mine to rub myself down vigorously, trying to restore some feeling in my limbs.

Once I'm mostly dry and recovered, I tell Maddox, "We need some food to warm us up. I think I've got some...oh crap, with the power out, I guess our options are kind of limited."

Wrapping the towel around his lower body, Maddox grabs the flashlight and we head to the small kitchen in my apartment. After digging through the cabinets, Maddox shines the light on his pile of plunder on the counter. "So, it looks like our options are two packs of Pop-Tarts, half a bag of chips, and some SlimFast bars. Why do you have SlimFast bars?" Maddox snorts.

"They're my roommates, but they're actually really good," I reply as I grab one of the chocolate bars from him. "I've got all kinds of stuff I could make, once the power comes back on. We can make do with this for now."

"If you say so," Maddox says, casting a skeptical eye at our supplies. He starts to dig into the bag of chips, when a loud crashing from outside my apartment startles him so badly he drops the sack.

"Was that thunder?" I gasp. I'm pretty sure it wasn't, which is more terrifying to me than the actual storm outside.

"No," Maddox whispers. He grabs the flashlight and my hand, then leads me back to my bedroom. "It sounded like a door breaking. I'm going to get dressed and go check it out. You hide out here, okay?"

"Fuck that," I hiss. "I'm coming with you. I know everyone on this hall, but you're a stranger. Someone might think you're a, ah, I don't know, a looter or something." As we're quietly arguing, I scramble back into my pajamas, while Maddox just pulls on his jeans and his leather cut.

Once we're dressed, he leads me to the front door, motioning for me to stand back as he cracks it open and peeks outside. "Do you see anything?" I whisper. I slap a hand over my mouth when Maddox holds a finger up to his lips, just as the beam of a flashlight briefly illuminates the hallway.

"You see anything else in there?" a coarse voice calls out from down the hall.

"Nah, it's clean. You get that television in the van okay?" someone says, so close to my doorway, I inadvertently gasp.

"Yeah, I got it," the first man responds, much closer now. "Let's check the rest of this hallway."

Maddox steps back from the door, digging inside his leather cut as his free hand waves at me frantically, pointing me back down the hall of my apartment. He pulls something out of an inner pocket of his vest as I duck behind the kitchen island.

I manage to hide just in time, as the door to my apartment swings open only a second later. "Look at this shit," the voice from the hallway says. "Crazy bitches took off without even closing the door."

A beam of light shines throughout the apartment, reflecting off of the kitchen appliances just over my head. They can't see me yet, but as soon as they come into the living room, I'll be completely exposed.

"Hitting up these apartments near a chick school was a great idea," the other voice agrees. "We've got this entire building to ourselves!" he exclaims as he steps into my apartment.

"Not exactly," I hear Maddox say, just before there is the sickening crunch of bone breaking, and the beam from the flashlight spins around before abruptly going out.

I peek around the edge of the kitchen island to see the first man who stepped into my apartment lying face down on the floor, his arms splayed out to the sides and his knees folded under him, so that his ass is sticking up in the air. The flashlight he was holding rolls across the floor as Maddox charges out into the hallway.

"Shit, shit, shit!" the other man shrieks as Maddox rams him into the wall outside my door. I scramble to my feet and rush over just in time to see Maddox slam his fist repeatedly into the man's face, which quickly becomes misshapen and unrecognizable. With a guttural roar, Maddox pulls the man forward and then slams his head back into the wall, so hard that the sheetrock crumples and dust rains down as the looter slumps to the ground.

"Jesus, Maddox, are you okay?" I cry as I rush to him. He's gasping for breath, his bare chest heaving under his leather cut. He turns to me and then shakes his right hand, before tugging off what looks like a metal plated fingerless glove. Glancing at the two men sprawled on the floor, I ask, "What is that?"

"Riding glove," he explains, wiping the metal plated knuckles on his jeans. "Got a steel backing to protect my hands. They're good for other stuff too," he adds, gesturing to the men on the ground. Tucking the glove back into his cut, he walks past me and grabs the man in my apartment by the ankles, then drags him out into the hall.

I gape at the bloody smear left by the man's face as Maddox pulls him clear of the door. "Oh my god, are they dead?" I gasp.

Maddox shakes his head as he crouches down and begins feeling around the man's pockets. "Nah, but they're fucked up. They deserve it for pulling this shit. Go grab your phone and call nine-one-one. I'll make sure they don't have any weapons on them in case they wake up. Tell them to send an ambulance too."

"I'll try," I agree. "I don't know if there is anyone to send, though. The news said two days ago that there would be no emergency services during the evacuation period. Their exact words where 'anyone who stays is on their own.'"

"And you decided to stay anyway?" Maddox sighs. "Man, I'm glad War sent me."

"Are you being sarcastic?" I demand. "How the hell could I have expected something like this?"

"There are always looters during national disasters," he replies. "But no, I'm not being sarcastic. I am glad War sent me. Meeting you has been amazing, and I hate to think what might have happened if they had found you here alone."

"Oh. Well, let me get the phone," I tell him, slightly mollified by his explanation. Just hearing Maddox say that meeting me has been amazing is giving me the strangest fluttering in my belly. That, combined with the shock and fear of what just happened, make me momentarily forget how terrified I am of the phone as the storm continues to rage outside.

I walk back from my bedroom, holding the phone away from me, after setting it to speaker. After only a couple of rings, an automated message answers, saying, "*Due to the mandatory evacuation of New Hanover County, emergency police, fire, and medical services have been temporarily suspended. If you need immediate assistance and are in a life-threatening situation, you may attempt to contact Pender County Emergency Management by calling...*"

I disconnect the call and toss the phone on the kitchen island, right by the pile of food we recently abandoned. "Well that was a bust." I sigh. "What the hell are we going to do with those guys?"

"I've got an idea," Maddox says. "Can you run downstairs and see if you can find the vehicle these keys go to?" he asks me as he holds out a keyring. "I found them in this guy's pocket. When I was on my way down here, I saw the National Guard setting up down near the mall. I can throw these dumb bastards into their ride, and then go drop them off with the Guardsmen. They're stationed out here to prevent shit like this from happening."

"That's dangerous! The storm is awful, and what if they wake up or something while you're driving?" I protest.

"It's less dangerous than letting them wake up outside your door. Honestly, I think they're going to need some medical attention. This first dude I hit, his jaw is shattered," Maddox says as he points to the man. Grabbing my flashlight from the kitchen, he clicks it on and points it at the second man in the hall. "This guy's even worse," Maddox explains, shining the light on the man's arms, which are twitching feebly in front of him. "I'm pretty sure that's a sign of brain damage."

"All right, but I don't know if I can go outside." I shudder as thunder rolls and rumbles outside. "I'll go to the front door and see if this key fob lights up a vehicle. Be right back."

I tiptoe past the two men lying in the hallway and jog down the stairs, already clicking the "panic" button on the key fob to see if any vehicle will respond before I have to get anywhere near the outer doors. Fortunately, as soon as I reach the bottom of the steps, I see a white cargo van has been backed up to the glass double doors leading into the lobby of my building. As the horn begins to beep and the lights flash, I see these two idiots didn't just back their van up to the doors, they actually backed right through them!

"I'm glad we took a break when we did," I tell Maddox when I get back upstairs. "These two drove their van right through the glass doors on the first floor, and were loading it up from there. If we hadn't stopped for a snack, we might not have heard them coming!"

"If we had been in Raleigh," Maddox grunts, as he heaves one of the limp forms over his shoulder, "we definitely wouldn't have heard them, and I wouldn't have to haul these dumb bastards out into a hurricane." Despite the harsh words, he is grinning at me as he straightens, and leans over to steal a kiss. "You seem to have a talent for getting into trouble," he adds, "so it's a good thing I decided to stick around."

"Get back as quickly as you can," I tell him, unable to choke down the nervous lilt in my voice. "I was certain I would be fine here alone, but now…"

"Hey, don't worry." Maddox winks at me. "Get inside and lock the door. I'll be so quick, you won't even have time to miss me."

I close and lock my door as Maddox begins laboriously hauling the two men down the stairs. Despite his reassurance, as the shock of what just happened begins to fade away, I start trembling violently. Another flash of lightning from outside paired with an immediate boom of thunder rattles my windows, sending me scurrying back to my bedroom. I dive under the covers and curl into a ball, praying for Maddox to return safely, but also thankful he can't see me as my childhood terror finally overwhelms me.

...

Maddox

"Quit whining," I grunt, as I toss the second looter down in the back of their cargo van. He's the one with the broken jaw, and he hasn't stopped moaning since he regained consciousness halfway down the stairs.

LANE HART & D.B. WEST

Once I drop him by his partner, I take a look around the back of their van. There are all sorts of electronics strewn haphazardly around. It looks like they were primarily trying to steal game consoles and televisions, but there are a couple of computers and guitar cases piled in here too. I find a wad of bungee cords tucked into a panel on the rear door, and after only a few moments, I have both of my new friends safely restrained.

The one whose head I almost put through the wall is still unconscious, but the first fellow with the broken jaw is wide awake and staring at me in bug-eyed horror. He's still trying to say something, but I knocked his lower jaw out of socket and he's completely unintelligible. "Shut up," I reiterate sternly as I slam the cargo van's rear doors.

Once I'm in the driver's seat, I crank up the van, then look back to make sure my passengers aren't trying to escape. I took both their wallets, so I know the one who is awake and grunting at me is named Dwayne. "We're going for a ride, boys. Dwayne, if you try anything, I swear to god, I'll drive this van straight into the ocean, you understand?"

He grunts something that sounds like agreement, so I drop the van into gear and then carefully drive it back out of the entryway of the apartment complex and right into the teeth of the hurricane.

"How the hell did you two even get here in this mess?" I ask conversationally, not expecting any reply. "Even with the wipers on full, I can't see a damn thing. How desperate or stupid do you have to be to go out and risk your ass in something like this?"

"Hell, I should probably ask myself that question, out here driving you two dumb sons-of-bitches around," I add, realizing that if I get the van up past twenty miles per hour, I'm completely blinded by the rain. "I should just throw you two into a ditch and let the storm take care of you," I grumble before falling silent and focusing on driving.

For the next twenty minutes, the only sounds I hear are the furious swiping of the windshield wipers and intermittent sobbing from the back of the van. I'm thoroughly miserable, but there is one upside to the entire situation—at least I know exactly where I'm going. I breathe a heavy sigh of relief as I finally spot a well-lit brick gatehouse on the road in front of me, just outside the local National Guard barracks.

As I pull up to the gate arm, a soldier in a poncho appears in the doorway of the guardhouse. I roll down the van window and flinch at the deluge of rain that washes over me. The soldier stands motionless for a moment, studying me, then yells, "State your business!"

"I caught two looters who broke into the apartment building where I was staying!" I yell back to him.

"You caught looters? Are they in the van?" the soldier calls back, still not leaving the shelter of the doorway.

"Yes!" I yell back as I wipe at my face. "They broke into a bunch of apartments and were loading this van up with things they stole. When they broke into the apartment I was in, I smacked them around and tied them up. They need medical attention, and to be locked up until the police can take over."

"Stay there," the soldier orders before disappearing back into the guardhouse. I roll up the window and look into the back of the van, trying to see if one of my "passengers" might have had the foresight to steal a towel. I don't see anything I can use to dry my hair, but I do spot the two looters, both now sitting up with their backs pressed against the rear doors, as far from me as they could scoot. The one with the broken jaw is crying and moaning, while the other simply stares at me in slack-jawed disbelief. Well, it's either disbelief or brain damage. I don't really care which.

When the soldier appears in the door of the gatehouse again a few minutes later, I roll the window back down. The van rocks as an even more powerful wave of wind and water sweep over me. I can see the soldier's lips moving, but his words are lost in the howling maelstrom.

"What did you say?" I roar at him.

"The MP's are on the way," he yells back at me. "They'll take over until the local authorities return." The next gust of wind staggers the soldier so badly that he disappears back into the guardhouse, his poncho almost torn from his body. I quickly roll up the window and turn back around to the looters.

"Hear that, boys? You're going to be guests of the local military police until the civilian cops get back. You two don't look like you served, so this should be an eye-opening experience for both of you." Broken-jaw sobs a little harder, while the other simply keeps staring at me blankly. Yup, that's definitely a concussion, at the least.

When the headlights of a large and imposing truck cut through the blinding rain and pull up on the other side of the gate arm, I turn the van off and step outside, my cut flapping around me until I wrangle it down and zip it over my bare chest. Four men pile out of the truck, all of them also wearing military ponchos.

One of them motions for me to follow him into the guardhouse, and I gladly comply. Once we're all crowded into the small brick building, the four men lower their hoods to reveal their helmets and faces. Looking over the four soldiers, I'm not sure if they really need head protection. They're so big, their skulls look bulletproof.

"Are we to understand that this civilian has apprehended some looters in the storm?" the man, who I presume is the lead MP, asks.

I'm not sure if he's talking to me, but I reply anyway. "Um, yeah...sir. Yes, sir, I mean," I add, as he turns his beady-eyed glare on me.

"Get a report!" the MP barks to one of his subordinates. The guardhouse soldiers scramble and produce a clipboard, along with some sort of official-looking paperwork, which they quickly fill out as I recount my story.

"That's the gist of what happened," I conclude a few minutes later. "I tied them up and loaded them into the van, along with all the things they stole, and brought them over here for you boys to take care of until they can be, uh...dealt with formally, I guess."

"And you can confirm this is your name and phone number?" the guardhouse soldier asks as he hands me the slightly soggy paperwork he had filled out.

"Yup, that's me, Maddox Holmes. That's my number," I confirm.

"All right, thank you for assistance in this matter," the lead MP says with a slightly softer tone. "I see by your patches, you're one of those Savage Kings' boys. I've heard of a few men who served that ride with you all. I'm glad you were around to help."

"Thank you," I reply, almost bashfully. Something about this man reminds me of War, and words of praise from him make me almost as uncomfortable. "So, ah, the keys and the dudes are in the van. I guess I'll leave you boys to it." I turn around to the doorway, only then realizing I might have a slight problem getting back to Audrey's.

The MP's are all chuckling as I turn back around. I can feel the flush in my face as I ask, "One of you boys mind maybe giving me a ride home? Bit of a walk on a day like this."

"Corporal, take the Humvee and get this man home. Then come straight back. Privates, you two climb into that van and secure the prisoners. I'll drive."

"Sir, yes, sir!" the corporal barks, before turning and immediately walking out the door. I give the remaining troops a nod as I follow him outside to the Humvee idling nearby, then stand awkwardly in the driving rain, trying to figure out how to get into the damned thing. It's jacked up high, and every time I try to look up to find a door handle, I'm completely blinded by the rain.

Thankfully, the corporal climbs around inside and cracks the door for me after a moment, then moves back to the driver's seat as I scramble inside.

"Thanks, man," I gasp as I finally slam the door shut. The gate arm raises almost immediately, and the Humvee lurches into motion.

"It's no trouble," the corporal replies once we clear the base. "I'm glad to have something to do, honestly. We were busy the first couple of days, making preparations around the city, but now we're pretty much confined to quarters while we wait this thing out."

"Ever had anybody bring in looters before?" I ask.

"Not like this, no." He laughs. "We've had to round some up before, sure, after they've been smacked around by a homeowner or something, but no one's ever tied them up and brought them to us."

"Well, you know how it is staying at an apartment. Didn't really have the storage space to keep them for a few days. Hey, just out of curiosity, since you're an MP, do you think I could be in any kind of legal trouble for roughing those guys up?"

"I didn't see them, but we'll get them evaluated on base and take care of them. Honestly, even if you had killed them, I doubt there would be any charges, since they came into your girlfriend's home. This is a castle doctrine state."

"Eh, she's not my 'girlfriend,' really..." I hedge, not sure how to really describe Audrey.

"Well, you were an invited guest, protecting her. They certainly weren't," the MP states. "You're navigator, so give me some directions while I concentrate on this road. If you want to talk, we can do it once we're there."

I laugh at his bluntness, then spend the rest of the ride giving him directions. Getting back takes almost twice as long in the Humvee. I have no idea if the MP is just that careful, or if the damned thing is just that slow.

Once we pull back up to the shattered glass front of the apartment building, the MP whistles in admiration. "Damn, they really did a number on this place."

"Yeah, this building had a first-floor lobby where all the mailboxes were set up on the walls. They plowed right through this place. I'm sure the other residents are going to be thrilled when they see this mess."

"It's flooding in there," the MP observes. "Are you guys going to be safe here?"

"Yeah, we're up on the higher floors," I reassure him. "Thanks again for the ride. Be safe on the way back, you hear?"

"Here, take this." The MP hands me a flashlight. "Take care," he tells me with a nod and a grin before I muscle open the heavy door of the truck and climb down. I run back inside as the lights from the Humvee wash over me briefly. He turns the truck around, then I stand in the darkness of the lobby, dripping and shivering as water surges around my boots.

I click on the flashlight he gave me and shine the beam around the first floor of the complex. Several doors on either side have been kicked open, and on a whim, I wander over to one of the open apartments near the stairwell. Shining the flashlight inside, I can see that its layout is similar to Audrey's. I step inside to scan the kitchen, breaking into a huge grin as I see what's sitting on the countertop.

Once I'm loaded up with my ill-gotten gains, I climb the stairs and use my boot to knock on Audrey's door. "Audrey, it's me, Maddox! Honey, I'm home!" I call.

I step back from the door once I hear the chains rattling, then break into a huge grin as Audrey throws open the door and rushes me. "Whoa, easy there, cowgirl, I come bearing gifts!" I laugh when she rushes me with her arms out, her hug threatening to cause me to drop everything I'm holding.

"God, I was so worried!" Audrey gushes. "I should have tried to come with you, but with the storm, and everything...what do you have?" she trails off, stepping back and shaking her now damp arms as she stares at me.

"I took a peek inside some of the apartments downstairs to, uh, 'assess the damage' from the looters. It turns out, that on top of stealing the folks in one-twenty-two F's television, those dastardly villains also swiped this entire chocolate cake and these two bottles of wine! At least, that will be the official version. Only you and I will know the terrible truth..."

Audrey's laughter interrupts me as she takes the cake pan from me, and I follow her back into the apartment with the two bottles of wine. While Audrey takes the cake to the kitchen and digs out a knife, I securely lock the door with the deadbolt and chain.

"I don't have any wineglasses," she says, digging through her cupboards. While her back is turned, I take off my cut, hanging it from the back of a barstool, then peel off my soggy boots and pants. "Oh!" She gasps in surprise as she turns back to see me standing in her kitchen, naked. "And you have no pants. Ok, then, it's going to be that kind of party!"

"We don't need wineglasses where we're going," I growl as I swipe a finger through the chocolate frosting, then rub it on her neck. I bend down to lick it up, sending a shiver through her body. She steps back from me to peel her tank top over her head, but when she tosses it down, instead of hitting the floor, it drapes over my erection, bobbing at her like a friendly ghost in the shadowy kitchen.

She bursts into laughter as she bends down to scramble out of her pajama pants, and I reach over to grab the bottle of wine. "Shall we take this to the bedroom?" she asks coyly as she straightens and puts her hands on her hips, flaunting her nudity at me.

"Bring the cake," I reply, turning to walk down the hall, her tank top leading the way, like a flag of conquest waving us on new sexual adventures.

CHAPTER FIVE

Audrey

DAYS LATER, MADDOX AND I ARE CUDDLING IN BED WITH ME tucked under his arm when I say, "So, tell me more about the MC."

I can feel his entire body tense up before he responds.

"I've told you all there is to know about it."

"Your father that you never got to meet was the one who started it?" I ask.

"Ah, yeah," Maddox replies. "And that's another thing that you can't tell your brother."

"Why not?" I push myself up on my elbow so that I can see his face better, even if it is pretty dark in here.

"Because he doesn't know that I'm Deacon's son," he explains. "Only one of the Savage Kings knows and that's because it was his job to dig into my background. The rest...well, I didn't want them to treat me differently, or think I was out to try and stake my claim to his legacy or whatever. I just wanted to learn about the man he was, and then I wanted to be a part of the club he left behind."

"I think I can understand that," I tell him. "Guess everyone has

53

their own secrets that they keep for one reason or another. What I don't understand is why War never told me about the Savage Kings."

"He was probably just trying to protect you."

"Maybe," I reply.

"And you never saw his cut?"

"Nope," I answer. "I know he has a motorcycle that he keeps covered in the garage but that's it. War's always been super protective and yeah, a little secretive now that I think about it, but I let him have his space because he took on raising me after our parents died."

"So, are you going to ask him about the MC now that you know?" Maddox inquires while stroking his hand up and down my spine. "'Cause, I mean, he didn't tell me not to mention the club or whatever, so you won't be screwing me over if you do."

"Yeah, I think I will the next time I see him face-to-face, you know? If I ask him on the phone, it'll be easier for him to blow me off."

"That's probably a good idea," he agrees. "Just remember not to bring up us doing this or not making it to Raleigh."

"I won't," I tell him.

"Oh, and the part about who my father is. Probably don't want to terrorize him with tales of looters and fighting either."

"Right," I agree.

"I've never told anyone about Deacon." Maddox sighs. "Reece, our club's IT guy, found the documents, but we didn't discuss it, other than for me to beg him to keep his mouth shut. I never got a chance to know my father but being around the Savage Kings makes me feel closer to him. That probably sounds crazy..."

"No, I get it," I tell him. "That's one of the reasons I was so eager to leave our home in Texas after we lost our parents. War wanted to move here for a job opportunity a guy from the Army offered him. And I wanted to escape the house we grew up in because it felt like the ghosts of my mom and dad were still there, but not in a good way."

"You lost two people who were a huge part of your life, so being there without them must have been hard," Maddox says. "I'm chasing a ghost while you were running from them."

"Exactly," I tell him.

"I want to tell the guys at the club, and I will, just as soon as I patch in," he says. "Then, maybe they can tell me more stories about the man I never got to meet."

"That will be nice," I agree.

"Chase and Torin, the vice president and president, are my cousins. That is, if they believe me and don't think I'm making up some shit, trying to cause problems."

"I seriously doubt anyone would think that about you," I tell him. Based on what I know about him already, he doesn't seem like the kind of guy who would do something like that.

"Maybe that's one reason why I'm nervous about speaking up," he says with a sigh. "But it would be really nice to actually have family again. Seems like I've been alone for years now. I haven't spoken to my mom since I graduated from the academy. Even while I was there, I only saw her maybe three times a year. I'm still too angry to look at her."

It's hard to imagine someone willingly avoiding one of their living parents when I would give anything to see mine again.

"You have every right to be angry at your mother. She should have told you who your father was and let you meet him," I agree. "But if you never forgive her, then you'll lose out on the years you could've had with her."

"Yeah," he agrees. "She's probably been worried sick about me, since I left graduation without saying goodbye or telling her where I was going."

"When was that?" I ask.

"A little over three years ago."

"Jesus, Maddox!" I spring up into a sitting position. "She probably thinks you're dead!" I tell him. "You should call her. Now."

"Says the woman who didn't want me to use the phone while it's storming outside," he mutters with a grin.

"After the storm is over then," I tell him. "Please?"

"I'll think about it," he agrees.

"No more sex unless you promise me that you'll call her," I tell him, while pointing my index finger at his bare chest. His, smooth, sexy chest that almost has me taking back my threat.

"Fine!" Maddox eventually agrees before he reaches up and pulls me back down on him. Then he rolls us over so that he's on top. "Now I know why men do whatever crazy shit women want just to keep them happy," he says as he lowers his lips to mine for a soft kiss. "You give them a taste of heaven, and then lock them out until you get what you want."

"You have us all figured out," I tell him with a grin.

"And you used sex to get a better grade?" he asks.

"Yeah," I answer. "I mean, the reason I got behind in the first place was because of afternoon thunderstorms."

Pulling back to see my face, he says, "You didn't go to class because it was storming?"

"Well, yeah."

"Did you try and explain that to the professor?" he asks.

"No."

"Why not? If he was a decent guy, then I'm sure he would've understood."

"No, he wouldn't," I reply. "He would think it was some bullshit excuse, and then I would've been screwed."

"So, you screwed him instead," Maddox responds.

"Right. And it worked. Just like I knew that it would."

"What if he had reported you?" he asks.

"Maddox, I'm not a complete idiot. I wouldn't have propositioned him if I hadn't seen his chubby bulging in the front of his slacks."

"Oh," he mutters, brow furrowing. "Is that why you propositioned me? You knew I would cave, and you would get what you wanted? To stay here?"

"Yes, and I was right with you, with my professor, and the police officer. Oh, and my landlord."

Pushing himself up until there's more space between us and he's straddling me, Maddox sits back on his heels and says, "What's this about a police officer and the landlord?"

"I was going thirty miles over the speed limit," I explain. "Forget the ticket, the cop threatened to take my license!"

"You had sex with him too?" he asks, the disapproval dripping off of his words.

"He was single and willing," I say. "And what's with the judging? If I were one of the...the guys in the MC sleeping with a bunch of 'club sluts,' you would offer me a fist bump, right? But because I'm a small, delicate woman, who looks sixteen instead of twenty-two, I'm supposed to wait until I'm married?" I scoff. "I am so sick of the double standard that women aren't supposed to have sex, but men can? I mean, come on!"

"I'm not judging because of the sex," Maddox tells me.

"But you are judging me."

"I just think that sleeping with people to get what you want is a little..."

"Slutty?" I supply for him when he pauses.

"No, I didn't say that," he scoffs.

"So, then what did you mean?"

Running his fingers through his messy brown hair, he says, "You shouldn't have to screw men to get your way. If you had just told me about your phobia, then I probably would've caved. And your professor most likely would have given you a break."

"What about the police officer?" I ask. "Or my landlord? I pleaded my case with both of them, and it got me nowhere. They didn't give a shit about me or my feelings! All they wanted was a quick fuck with no strings attached."

"Did you even want them?" Maddox asks.

"Of course. I wouldn't sleep with some gross guy. Yuck."

LANE HART & D.B. WEST

Scrubbing his palm over his face, he asks, "Why did you think you had to sleep with the landlord?"

"Because he was going to make me get rid of Stella."

Lowering his hand, Maddox says, "The cat?"

"Pets aren't allowed here," I explain.

"And you knew that before you got Stella?"

"Yes."

"So then why..."

"Because I was lonely, and I wanted a friend," I respond. "My roommate is a real bitch."

"And you told the landlord that, but he still said hell no?" he guesses.

"Yep," I answer. "And since War is paying for this place, I couldn't exactly ask him to move me into someplace that allows pets."

"So, you got a cat, knowing you weren't allowed to have it, and then slept with the landlord?" Maddox summarizes.

"I did. Look, I had the hots for him anyway, the discussion we had about the cat just...opened some doors. It was a casual thing, which I'm sure you understand."

Maddox lets out a soft sigh as I shift underneath him, getting more comfortable while also grinding myself against his rapidly thickening cock.

"I'm still having trouble imagining my brother as part of this 'Savage Kings,'" I tell Maddox. "I mean, I don't know if I really believed you were the 'badass biker' type until you messed those guys up. I've seen some fistfights before, but what you did...that was an entirely different level of violence, you know? Does War do things...like that?"

Instead of replying, Maddox just stares at me, his eyes only inches away from mine. He searches my face while reaching up to brush my hair back behind my ear.

"What is it?" I ask him.

CHAPTER SIX

Maddox

Holy shit!

Why did it take me this long to see what Audrey is doing?

She's been playing me from the start, just like she played her professor, a police officer, and her fucking landlord!

The only difference is, she's played me for the long game because she didn't want to leave her apartment.

I get that her fear is serious, and I understand that it comes from a very shitty past where she lost her parents. But like I told her, if she had just explained all of that to me from the beginning, instead of lying about who she was and fucking me, then I would've let her stay here.

Probably.

Maybe?

Okay, so I'm not sure if I would've done that, or just grabbed her and ran out into the storm to get her inland. Guess now we'll never know.

The lights suddenly flicker back on in the bedroom, as if my epiphany was responsible for the surge.

"Yay! We have power!" Audrey says.

"Yay," I repeat, without any of her enthusiasm.

If the power is back on, then the conditions outside must have improved, which means I no longer need to stay here.

Moving off of Audrey, I find my boxer briefs I lost days ago, and start putting them on.

"What are you doing?" Audrey asks, when I reach for my jeans to pull them up my legs.

"Getting dressed," I reply, as if it's obvious. "If the power is on, then that means the storm is over and the roads are clear."

Going over to the window, I lift one of the blinds to peek outside over the top of her dresser. I have to squint because the sun is so bright. Tree limbs, leaves, and debris are scattered around the roads, yards, and on the vehicles, but the water has receded.

"You're leaving?" Audrey asks.

"Yeah," I respond.

Why am I dreading that so much? I should be angry at her for using me like every other man she comes across in life who doesn't automatically bend to her will. Instead, there's just this ache in my chest that wishes the power would've stayed off a little longer...

"I should get back and see how bad a shape the island is in," I tell her. "You want to call War and tell him we're 'back'?" I ask, using finger quotes around the last word since we were supposed to be in Raleigh.

"Okay," Audrey agrees. "I'll tell him that my roommate called and said the power was back on."

"Right," I agree, thinking she's pretty damn good at lying. I wonder how many other lies she's told her brother.

"Thanks for staying with me," she says.

"No problem," I reply as I slip on my T-shirt and then move the sleeping yellow kitten from my cut to put it on. After I'm dressed, I stand there and look at Audrey, still naked in bed, hair tussled from all the fun we had. But that's all it was—fun. Is that why I'm dreading leaving her? Because I'll miss the sex? That's probably all there is to it. I got attached because she was my first and second and third, and however many times we fucked in three days. It'll be impossible to forget her now, no matter how hard I try.

Even if she wasn't just sleeping with me to get her way and pass the time, it's not like I could keep coming to see her. Not without War finding out and then doing what he threatened—taking my cut and kicking my ass.

Now that it's time to leave, though, I can't figure out how to say goodbye. "See ya later" doesn't work because I *won't* be seeing her later, or ever again, since War makes a point of keeping his family separate from the MC. So instead, I just tell Audrey, "Thanks for everything."

"No, thank you, Maddox," she says before she jumps out of bed and then comes over to throw her arms around my neck, still completely naked. It's like she's trying her best to tempt me into tearing off my clothes and throwing her back in bed.

But I can't. Not this time.

So, I give her a brief hug and then push her away. "See ya." I say the stupid words, even though we both know they're bullshit.

"See ya, Maddox," Audrey replies, and then I make myself walk away from her.

...

Audrey

ONCE I HEAR the door close behind Maddox, I pick up Stella and cuddle her to my bare chest, then go into the living room to lock the door. When I turn back to the empty apartment, a weight sinks into my gut, a hollow aching that I know well. I put my cat down and go to the bathroom to start the shower, hoping that I'll be able to get some hot water.

As I sit on the edge of the tub, waiting for the freezing spray to pass, I feel a hot tear trickle down my cheek. I look around before swiping it away, irrationally worried that Maddox might burst back in and see it. I'm not upset about him leaving, and I didn't think that these last few days were turning into...something!

"Ugh, what the fuck!" I groan as I feel the water. I'm not sure if I'm referring to the fact that the shower is still freezing, or to the jumble of emotions whirling around inside me in a nauseating spin.

Giving up on the shower, I go back to my room to find my pajamas, then spend a few minutes cleaning up the apartment. Maddox and I spent most of the last few days in my room, but I do need to dispose of the wine bottles and cake pan, evidence of the little bit of looting he engaged in during the storm.

I break into a smile as I swipe a finger through the last bit of frosting still clinging to the pan and suck it off of my finger, remembering all the things that Maddox and I did together. Just the memories of him ease the ache in my guts, and I decide then and there that what we had was more than just a "nice time." I don't know what it is between the two of us yet, but I'm almost certain it wasn't one-sided. Now, I just have to figure out this whole "Savage Kings" business between my brother and Maddox, and if there is some way we can navigate it to find an honest future for all of us.

CHAPTER SEVEN

Maddox

I'M STROLLING DOWN THE BOARDWALK COLLECTING GARBAGE IN a trash bag, wasting time and thinking about someone I shouldn't be when my phone starts ringing in my cut pocket.

"Shit," I mutter to myself.

Tossing the garbage bag down, I pull the phone out and glance at the screen.

Usually I answer as soon as I see War's name, but after sleeping with his sister for three days, I've been trying really hard to avoid him since I got back to Emerald Isle. He thinks the two of us were in Raleigh because I lied to him. He would kill me if he knew that I stayed in bed with his sister during the hurricane after the entire coast was evacuated.

When the phone stops buzzing for a few seconds before it starts up again, I cave and finally hit the green button to take the call.

"Yes, sir?" I answer.

"Where the hell are you?" War snaps. "I thought you were back in town."

"Ah, yeah, I am back in town."

"Then get your ass to the clubhouse!" he shouts through the phone line. "You're holding up our meeting."

"What?" I ask in confusion.

"Our meeting was supposed to start ten minutes ago, and we've been looking for you!"

"A Savage Kings' meeting?" I ask for clarification.

"No, Mad Dog, our Girl Scout meeting," he huffs. "We're counting to see who sold the most cookies."

"Huh?" I mutter.

"Get your ass to the chapel!" he yells before hanging up.

That's when I realize War was being sarcastic, making a joke. He never makes a joke. And I very rarely get invited to a Kings meeting.

"Fuck!" I shout as I take off running as fast as my legs can carry me back to the Savage Asylum. Is today finally the day I'm gonna get my patch? If so, I picked the worst fucking day to go wandering off just to avoid facing my sponsor.

I rush into the bar, punch in the code to get to the basement, and hold on to the railing to take the steps three at a time to get to the bottom. Then, it's just a quick sprint to the open door, where our VP Chase Fury is waiting with a bucket in his hands.

"Phone," Chase says as soon as my boots skid to a halt in front of him. I lower my eyes from his face after staring at him for a moment. I don't want him thinking I'm into dudes when I'm just looking for any family resemblance...

I raced over with my burner still in my hand, so I toss it into the plastic container.

"Get inside," he tells me. "Everyone's waiting, and we all have shit to do."

"Right, sorry," I say, as I enter the room I've only been inside a handful of times. I look around at the long wooden table where all the brothers are waiting with their angry gazes on me, especially War. And I'm a little disappointed that there's still only one empty seat, which belongs to Ian, their brother in prison, not me.

"Sorry," I say to everyone again.

Damn. Does this mean I'm not getting my patch? Wait, did War find out about me and Audrey, and tell the MC? Am I here for some type of punishment?

"Find a spot against the wall so we can get started," Torin, our president and my unknowing cousin, says to me as Chase comes into the room and shuts the door, leaving the phone bucket outside. The guys take their privacy seriously.

"Yes, sir," I agree, going over to the wall on the far side of the table to prop myself up out of the way, anxious to find out what's going on.

"We're gonna sandwich in the bad news between the good," Torin starts, then a smile splits his face. "So, first of all, thank you all for asking about Lexi and my new daughter, Kensi. They're both home and doing great. It was Lexi's idea to give her part of Kennedy's name and her own..."

"Glad to hear it," Coop says, as all the guys cheer and slap their palms on the table.

"Congrats, boss, that's great news," Reece tells him.

"Thank you, brothers," Torin says with a nod. "And let's also congratulate War on his win in court yesterday."

"Congrats, man," Chase says, offering him a fist bump across the table, and the other guys follow suit.

"All right," Torin says. "Now, before War gives us the bad news, I want to ask everyone to stay calm."

Muttered curses can be heard around the table at that dismal warning.

"War?" Torin says. "Tell them what you know."

"Yeah," War agrees with a nod. "I hate to be the one to break this news to you, but I've just learned that the feds have launched an investigation into the Kings."

Oh shit.

"What the fuck?" someone shouts, most likely Chase, immediately followed by more curses.

War holds up his palms for silence before he goes on to say, "I don't know much more than that, but I don't need to tell you all that this is some serious shit. We don't have details of what they're looking for or plan to accuse any of us of, but everyone needs to keep their noses spotless over the next few months. Be extremely careful about what you say and where you say it. Burner phones are a *must* for all club business. If you're a felon, don't even think of carrying a weapon other than your knife. Hell, you all need to even do the speed limit. Let's not give them a single excuse to take one of us in."

Torin jumps in, "Does anyone need a business card for the club's criminal attorney? I have a few extra, if so. Keep it on you in your wallet at all times. And if you get cornered or taken in, remember the cardinal rule, don't say a fucking word about anything to anyone. You ask for our lawyer, and that's it."

Everyone mutters their grumbled agreement.

"We'll let you know more as soon as we find out," War tells the brothers. "Reece will be working his magic, hopefully coming up with more info."

"I'll do my best, brother," Reece agrees with a tilt of his chin.

"Now, on to better news," Torin begins. "It looks like we may be losing our prospect soon..."

Everyone's head turns to look at me.

"Maddox, you've served long and hard for the MC, and we'll be taking a membership vote soon if you're still interested in joining," Torin declares.

"Really?" I ask. "Of course I want to join."

"Even with the federal shit hanging over our heads?" War asks.

"Fuck the feds," I say without hesitation, receiving a chorus of cheers for it.

"But if we lose our prospect, who's gonna wash our bikes and do all our grunt work for us?" Dalton asks with a smirk.

I flip him off with a grin of my own.

"That's why we need Maddox to work with Reece to find us a

suitable replacement prospect or two. There's a list of hang-arounds for you to go through and choose from," Torin informs us. "I want them thoroughly, and I mean, *thoroughly* vetted, Reece. I want to know everything about them, including every thought in their naïve little heads."

"You got it, boss," Reece agrees. "That polygraph machine is gonna come in real handy."

"Damn right," Torin says before he looks to me. "And Maddox, we want you on training duty. You won't be sponsoring these boys, but you will be in charge of overseeing our new recruits for the first few months. That will be your only job from now until the end of the year," Torin tells me. "I want you to haze them twice as hard as we hazed you, you hear me? See how much they can take and then give them some more. When they leave here, I want you up their asses, seeing where they go and who they know. You snoop through their phones, you listen to their calls, you pat them down head to toe for wires before they step foot in this clubhouse. Understood?"

"Yes, sir," I reply.

"Once we have our new prospects, we'll see about finding another chair for this table," Torin declares.

Thank fuck.

As soon as Torin slams his gavel down, adjourning our meeting, everyone gets up and starts filing out. Everyone except for War, who comes toward me.

"I know it's taken longer than you wanted to get here," he says while I try to force the eye contact, even though I feel awful for keeping such a huge secret from him. "But it's been chaos around here lately, so the guys are a little more cautious about who they trust. You should be too when it comes to the new prospects."

"Right, of course," I agree. "I'll make sure to do that."

"Good, that's good to hear," he says. "I have some...things to take care of over the next few days, but let's catch up over the weekend. There's something I want to discuss with you."

Gulp.

"Okay, sure," I agree.

With a slap to my shoulder, he says, "See you then."

CHAPTER EIGHT

Maddox

REECE GAVE ME THE CONTACT INFORMATION FOR FIVE
potential new prospects who had been hanging around the Kings
clubhouse the last few weeks, or even months. I knew just what I
wanted to do to put them through their paces and see exactly what
they were made of, and I let them all know to meet me at our strip
club, Avalon, on Friday night for their "initiation."

I had seen a couple of them ride by me toward the parking lot in
the back of the club as I stood out front, but the new recruits waited
until all five had gathered before coming around the building to face
me. As they approached me by the door, all five of them cast repeated
glances at the line of women standing behind a velvet rope, waiting
to be admitted to the club.

"Do any of you gentlemen know why I asked you here tonight?" I
ask them as they form a line in front of me.

They all glance at each other before casting their eyes down to
their boots. One of them, a guy named Carl, sheepishly says,
"No, sir."

"Do you want to hazard a guess?"

After a moment of silence, Mike, a young guy who only recently started hanging around the club asks hopefully, "You want us to work security, see how we handle ourselves?"

I snort a laugh at that. "You saw the clientele waiting to get in tonight. Do you think those rowdy ladies are going to need a firm hand to keep them under control?" Some of the women in line hear my comment and respond with catcalls and whistles at the young men standing with me.

"They're all women," the ginger, not the smartest of our potential recruits, observes. "Are there a bunch of lesbians in town?"

The ladies who overhear that question burst into laughter and sporadic boos, before I reply, "I'm not aware of any unusual amounts of lesbians in town this evening. Dumbass. No, Mike was partially right. Tonight, we're going to see how you handle yourselves. It's ladies' night here at Avalon, and you boys are going to be part of the show. Now, get your asses backstage and work with the performers to find some outfits. Don't worry if you don't like what you end up wearing, you won't have it on for long."

All five of them glance at each other and shuffle their feet as the women in line cheer. "Move your bitch asses!" I roar at the men, then step aside as they hustle into the building. "We'll see you inside, ladies, in just a few moments. Make sure to take good care of my young recruits!" I call to them as I follow along.

Once I'm inside, I almost run into the back of Pete, a skinny young man who had been coming into the clubhouse since he was old enough to drink. "I told you to move your ass, Pete," I growl at him.

"Dude, Maddox, I'm not sure about this..." he starts to protest.

"Then you're not sure you want to be a fucking King!" I yell. "You have to be willing to do anything to be a brother in this club, and if that means waving your anorexic cock in a lady's face, you rub it till it's chubby and you shake that fucking thing like it's your royal goddamn scepter! You understand me?"

Pete jerks straight up and damn near salutes me as he rushes to follow the rest of the boys to the back where the changing rooms are located. I can't help grinning as I head to the bar, waving over the muscled and oiled boy toy in a bow tie tending the drinks tonight.

"What can I get you, sir?" he asks me politely.

"Pour me a Jack and Coke," I reply, as I take a seat and watch the women begin filing into the tables scattered all around the stage.

"I love the way you handled that boy." The bartender grins after he pours the drink for me and slides it to me. "My crew loves coming to work your club, you always bring us the cutest little recruits. They didn't make you dance with us, did they? I'm sure I would remember you."

I'm not taken aback at all by the man hitting on me, I just laugh and reply, "You're right, I missed this experience when I was coming up in the club. I would have gladly done this compared to some of the other jobs they gave me."

"Really?" he drawls. "Most of those boys are so embarrassed when they get out here, they whine and moan like it's going to be the death of them. What other stuff did they make you do while you were trying out for the club that was so awful?"

"Prospecting," I correct him automatically, "although tryouts is a good way of looking at it. I had to do all sorts of stuff, but the absolute worst was when I had to clean out the septic tank at the clubhouse. I had to do it with a shovel. Don't think about that too hard," I caution him. "No matter how bad you're imagining, the reality was worse. So, so much worse."

"Uh-uh, baby, no way." The bartender waves me off. "You boys are crazy with that 'do anything for the club' business. Ain't nobody going to catch me shoveling poop."

"It was worth it," I tell him as I raise my glass in a toast. The bartender is already moving away to take more orders as the seats around me quickly fill with women eagerly awaiting the show.

I've never been to a "male review" before and I have to admit the experience is eye-opening, even for me. I've been around the girls at the clubhouse when they were partying and feeling frisky, but these ladies tonight are cutting loose and going absolutely wild. I cheer right along with them as my recruits take the stage, mingled between the real performers. I even make my way up to the stage to make it rain a few times when my boys clumsily attempt to mimic some of the professional maneuvers. By the end of the night, they even seem to be enjoying themselves. Well, all except for Pete who, it turns out, I was being generous too when I called his dick anorexic. That poor boy's unit is so turtled up when he gets down to his G-string that the women in the club yell for us to turn the heat up to see if we can coax the little guy out. They end up chasing him from the stage practically in tears, and I can't help but add my laughter to theirs.

I'm having a great time when a pretty young redhead, her pale cheeks flushed with alcohol, elbows her way to the bar right by my stool. Instead of trying to order a drink, though, she lays a hand on my knee and forces my leg to the side, then wedges herself close to me. She's so close, I can count the freckles on the upper slopes of her breasts, and smell the vodka she's been drinking when she breathlessly says, "How much for a dance with you, baby?"

"I'm not working tonight, honey," I reply politely, my good humor evaporating as a hard knot of guilt suddenly grips my stomach. "I'm just here to help make sure some of the younger talent doesn't try to run away tonight. There are plenty of other boys who will play with you," I assure her as I gently turn my stool and extract myself from her.

"Bah, you're no fun," she pouts before waving imperiously to summon the bartender. "You can always tell when one's taken, I should have spotted it right off."

"I'm not taken—" I start to protest, but quickly stifle myself. The guilt that is churning inside me begs to differ, and I realize...I miss Audrey. Desperately so, in a way I've never felt about anyone. I pick up my drink and finish it off in one swallow, then shake the glass as the bartender comes over to the redhead, signaling for a refill. I know

I can't feel this way about War's sister, but I have to glumly admit as I pick up my fresh drink, that she's taken root inside of me and being apart these last few days has only made this feeling, whatever it is, grow and swell inside of me.

CHAPTER NINE

Maddox

IT'S TAKEN WEEKS, UNFORTUNATELY, BUT REECE AND I HAVE narrowed down our potential prospects to four guys. We've put them through hell, and they still keep showing up for more punishment and humiliation. All except for Pete, that is, who realized after the debacle at Avalon that he, literally, didn't have the balls to be a member of the Kings.

Now, though, it's time to select the two guys who will get to wear the Savage Kings leather prospect cut.

Finally!

The faster I get them trained up and ready, the faster I'll get my patches.

"I think Mike and Cedric are our best picks out of the four," I tell Reece when we convene down in his apartment to discuss our potential recruits, who are waiting upstairs.

Grinning, he slaps my shoulder and says, "You're a natural at this, kid. Just like your old man."

"What do you mean?" I ask, wanting him to tell me more about Deacon since he's the only one who knows he was my father.

"I mean, you have the same intuition as he did about who can cut it as a King and who can't. That one boy, Carl, he wouldn't have lasted a day. And the ginger? He looked like he was ready to piss his pants. That's a pussy rat if I ever saw one."

"So, Deacon picked all the prospects?"

"When I was coming up, he did. He handpicked me," Reece says. "I was right out of the Army, had only been a hang-around for a few weeks, while some of the other guys had years on me. Still, Deacon chose me over them, said he knew I was a King by the way I held myself."

"Really?"

"Apparently, I looked like a stubborn son of a bitch who could take a punch and keep kicking ass."

Yeah, I could see that about him from the first time we met too.

"Torin is the one who picked me, and Cooper picked Holden," I say, and Reece nods.

"Torin's got the same eye as his uncle. He had watched some of the guys give you shit when you were a hang-around, and could tell that you bottled up your anger but weren't a hothead like Holden was. You keep your cool and play shit smart. He trusted you right off the bat, which is rare for Torin, even before Hector Cruz fucked him over."

"Why did he trust me?" I ask. "I was just a homeless kid who thought everyone saw me as a leech. And I didn't tell him the name I was born with..."

"Everyone has their secrets," Reece says. "And that's fine as long as those secrets won't screw over the MC. Yours isn't anything shameful or hurtful."

"You think he knew I was lying?" I ask.

"Maybe. But you held your own and didn't back down to anyone, even him. You may go around saying, *yes, sir* to the brothers, but we can all hear it in your tone and see it in your eyes—you think you're an equal to us, not a subordinate, and there's nothing wrong with that. We may make prospects do the grunt work, but we don't want pissant pussies. It takes a man with confidence and a little swagger to become a King."

"And you think I have confidence and swagger?" I ask with a grin.

"I said *a little*, don't be twisting my words," Reece mutters. "Now, if you're done talking about your feelings, let's go get rid of the trash and tell our boys the good news. I'll even let you do the honors."

On the way back up the steps, he says, "You've been a workhorse long enough, Mad Dog. Now it's time to start showing us what you're made of. Don't be scared of pissing anyone off. That vote of yours is as good as done."

"Thanks," I say on an exhale of relief before we get to the door at the top. Switching on the badass soon-to-be-King version of myself, I walk into the bar saying, "Look alive, wannabes. Two of you have made the cut."

The boys all straighten up as they form a line, standing shoulder to shoulder.

"If you think we decided that you're one of the two that has the balls it takes to be a prospect for the Kings, take a step forward," I tell them as I pace in front of the line. I pull out the big Ka-Bar knife War gave me from the holster and spin it around for them to all see it. "But, if you step up and you're wrong, we'll have to take one of your toes off before your dumb ass is sent out the door."

This is the final test to see if we've picked the right guys—not boys, but men brave enough to step up, even if there's a chance they'll face an incredible amount of pain.

After a few seconds of hesitation, Cedric finally mutters a curse but then takes a step forward. Riding his wave of confidence, Mike eases up beside him.

"That everyone who wants to be a King?" I ask. It's so quiet in the bar, I can hear crickets chirping outside. "All right, the rest of you out. Mike and Cedric, take off your shoes."

The two chumps run from the bar like their asses are on fire.

Cedric bends down to start untying his boots while Mike looks at me and licks his lips. "You're fucking with us, right?"

"Take your goddamn shoe off," Reece, who had been quiet, barks at him. "If he has to tell you again, he'll take two toes instead of one."

"Dammit," Mike huffs before he kneels down.

While their heads are both lowered, Reece reaches behind the bar and grabs the two leather cuts with prospect patches that were draped over a stool and tosses them to me. I throw one down on Cedric's shoulders and the other on Mike.

"Put your shoes back on and don't make us regret this decision, or you'll be losing more than a toe," I warn them, channeling my inner savage.

"Pussy training starts at four tomorrow afternoon at the salvage yard," Reece informs them. "Don't be late."

"Yes, sir. Thank you, sir," both guys say before they stand up and put on their cuts with grins splitting their faces.

I remember the day Torin gave me the one I'm wearing. He sent me and Holden on a scavenger hunt to find the cock-cycle. It was just as awful as it sounds. The two of us knew we were looking for a Harley, but had no idea until we spotted it that it was Chase's old rat bike...that was covered in dildos. Still, Holden and I fought for who would ride it, and I won. Pulling up in the clubhouse parking lot that night, with the guys waiting around at the bonfire, was fucking amazing. That's when Torin and War gave me my cut and War told me he wanted to be my sponsor.

It was one of the best days of my life. Before that, I knew it was possible they would never give me a chance to be one of them.

After hanging around for two years, I had seen a lot of guys come and go. Not to mention how terrifying it was to see Holden eventually meet his end.

Still, I didn't give up and it paid off.

Soon, I'm going to finally be a King.

CHAPTER TEN

Audrey

"You DO KNOW HOW TO WORK A DISHWASHER, DON'T YOU?" I ask Mindy, my wonderful roommate, when she comes into the kitchen and I'm cleaning her crusty macaroni pot from last night.

"I was gonna wash my shit if you had given me a chance," she grumbles.

"Yeah, right," I mutter. "And could you try not to slam doors when you come in after midnight?"

"You're such a nag," she huffs. "A slag nag."

Rolling my eyes at her insults, I finish cleaning the dishes and then grab my purse, keys, and phone to head out to the store. I need a few groceries for the weekend and Stella needs more cat food. I swear she eats as much as a lion.

Although, she hasn't been eating as much the last few weeks. I think she misses Maddox too, even though he was only in our lives for a short time before he disappeared.

And while I'm not completely sure, I think he was pissed the day he left. He didn't even ask for my phone number. I had created this grand fantasy in my head, where he would confront my brother Warren and profess his feelings for me, then demand to know how to contact me. When that didn't happen, I started imagining every time I heard footsteps in the hall, that it was Maddox, back with a cake and a bottle of wine. It never was, just our neighbors returning and the police coming through to get statements about the looters. I don't really know why I'm surprised. Have any of the other guys I've slept with wanted to see me again? No. At least, not unless it was to fuck.

Speaking of which, my shitty day gets even better when I'm picking out fruit in the produce section and a man steps up next to me.

"Hello, stranger."

Ugh, Professor Burrows. While he's nice to look at—tall and lean but still muscular, with shaggy dark hair and facial hair to make him look more distinguished—he was a selfish lover. While I was hoping for a one-and-done to keep from failing his class, he would always hold the power to change my grade back if I failed to fuck him whenever he wanted for the rest of the semester. He always enjoyed himself, but it wasn't much fun for me. Not like when I was with Maddox...

"Hi," I reply, while adding a few more peaches to my plastic bag.

"I see you endured the summer."

"I did," I agree.

"Looking forward to starting your senior year?"

"I am," I reply, eager to get my Marine Biology degree to escape the all-girl campus and work in one of the local aquariums.

He takes a step closer to me so that the front of his body is pressed against my side and one particular part of him is hard against my hip. "I've heard you're taking Professor Talbot's Organic Chemistry class. That's a tough one, and you and I both know that science isn't your strong suit."

"I'm sure I'll be fine," I say, stepping away from him.

"Talbot's a good friend. A real good friend," he says again for emphasis. "In fact, we tell each other everything, you know, share notes on students."

"Good for you," I reply.

"He can't wait to meet you."

"Yeah, same here," I mutter. "Anyway, I have to get going, but it was good seeing you," I lie before I grab my buggy and hurry away to the checkout, even though I only have two of the ten things I needed on my grocery list. I'll just go to another store to get the rest, one where I hopefully won't run into any creepy professors who have seen me naked.

But once I'm in my car, I find myself driving back to my apartment. And once I'm there and hear Mindy's radio blaring with her god-awful hick music, I start packing my suitcase without a second thought.

I need a break from this place. The city, the apartment, and all the people here before classes start.

I can head home with the excuse that I want to spend some time with my nephew before school starts on Monday, and maybe even run into Maddox. But I really do want to spend time with Ren. I was worried sick about him and I'm so glad that Warren got him back.

My brother is always telling me to come home more often, and while he isn't fond of cats, once he sees Stella's cute fluffy face, I'm sure he'll love her and not mind her visiting too.

...

I SLIP my key into the lock on my brother's garage door and ease inside, closing it softly behind me before I set Stella down on the cement with my suitcase.

Warren's truck is here, so I know he's inside the house somewhere.

LANE HART & D.B. WEST

What I'm hoping is that I'll have a few minutes to look around before he realizes I'm here.

Going over to the black tarp draped over his bike, I quietly peel the plastic off until I can see every inch of the big, shiny black Harley. While I knew he had a bike because I had heard it on the street, and seen the tarp, I didn't know it was this damn nice. I mean, my brother deserves to be able to buy nice things for himself, it's just that I've felt guilty for the ten years I've had to depend on him. Especially the last three years of college when he's had to waste a ton of money on my apartment and tuition. If he can still afford a bike like this, then I'm wondering if he's earning more money at the auto shop than I thought.

Going around to the briefcase-looking satchel on the side of the bike, I pop it open and then reach inside to pull out a leather cut so similar to Maddox's, I even hold it up to my nose to get a whiff of his scent. Why didn't I ever notice this smell on my brother?

Unfolding the leather, I first find the "Sergeant-at-Arms" patch on the front before turning it around to examine the enormous white patches on the back. The bearded skull king is not anything I would expect my brother to wear.

"Come on, Stella. Let's go have a talk with Uncle Warren."

Still holding the leather cut, I step through the door that comes out in the kitchen and find the living room empty.

"Warren!" I start down the hallway. "Oh, brother where art thou?" I call out before I come to a stop in his bedroom doorway...and find him scurrying around the room with so much skin showing, I immediately turn my back. "Why are you naked at four o'clock in the afternoon?" I shout at him.

"Why didn't you tell me you were coming home?" he grumbles.

"It was going to be a surprise!"

"Sorry," he says.

At first, I'm assuming he's talking to me, until I hear a woman say, "It's okay. I've been wanting to meet Audrey, just with more clothes on."

"Nova?" I ask aloud without turning around when I recognize the social worker's voice. "You're sleeping with Nova?"

"Ah, yeah. We're seeing each other," War says from behind me. "We've been seeing each other, for a few weeks now, actually."

"Wow," I mutter in surprise since my brother hasn't talked to a woman, much less had one over, since the Marcie debacle.

"Could you give us a little privacy?" War asks when I refuse to budge from my spot in the doorway.

"I didn't see anything," I assure him. "And this can't wait." I hold up the leather cut by one finger and ask, "What is this?"

"Ah, where did you get that from?" my brother asks before he snatches it away from me. "First, you bust in on me without calling and now you've been going through my shit? Have you lost your damn mind?"

"Have you been lying to me?" I ask when I turn around to face him, glad to see he's dressed in jeans and a tee and that Nova is too. She's beautiful and tall and skinny, so I want to hate her, but I can't if she makes my brother happy.

"Did Maddox say something to you a few weeks ago?" Warren asks, making my eyes snap back to his narrowed golden ones.

"No, you don't get to be angry at someone else for telling me what *you* should have told me!" I declare. "Jesus, he showed up wearing a damned vest just like this! You're in a biker gang and you send a member to my house, not thinking that I might notice something odd?"

"It's a motorcycle club," he says before putting his arms through the cut. "And it's none of your business. Maddox should've kept his mouth shut! Or at least changed his clothes!"

"He was only trying to convince me that he knew you. What was I supposed to do when a random guy shows up at my door to pick me up? And it turns out, he knew you better than I did!"

"War..." Nova starts when she comes up beside my brother. "She's a grown woman. Don't you think she deserves to know?"

"Fine," Warren agrees. "Let's go talk in the living room."

"Okay," I say, glad that he's willing to talk instead of blowing me off. I guess I have Nova to thank for that.

"And this is your home. I'm not saying you have to call when you're coming, but a heads-up would've been...what the fuck is that!" Warren yells when he stumbles into the hallway wall because Stella was rubbing on his leg.

"I got a kitten," I explain, reaching down to grab her and pick her up in my arms. "Isn't she cute? Her name is Stella."

"What are you doing with a cat? You can't have pets in your apartment!" Warren grumbles.

"Ah, well, I talked to Joe and he said he's okay with Stella." I leave off the bit about what I had to do to convince him. Besides, I liked it. We would probably still be going at it if he wasn't allergic to cats. And if I hadn't met Maddox...

"Really?" Warren asks in disbelief.

"Really. Call him and ask him if you don't believe me," I tell him. "I'm actually telling the truth, unlike you." It's a low blow but he deserves it. "Where's Ren? Still at daycare while you get naked at four in the afternoon?"

"He loves his teachers and missed the kids," Warren huffs. "He asked to go back until kindergarten starts, so that's where he is for another half hour."

"I'm not judging," I tell him when I flop down on the sofa. "I just want answers. What's with the MC?"

"Fine," Warren mutters. "I moved here to join the Savage Kings. That's where I've been working for the past six years."

"You work in their garage?" I ask, and he trades a look with Nova who gives a supportive nod.

"Not exactly," he replies. "I help oversee their businesses and watch out for the president. In exchange for being a member, I get a portion of the business profits."

"The MC owns businesses?" I ask.

"Yes, several that are very lucrative."

"And that's how you afford...everything?"

"Yes."

"Is it dangerous?" I inquire and again he trades a look with Nova who gives another nod of encouragement.

"Sometimes," Warren finally answers through clenched teeth. "That's why I have a million-dollar life insurance policy, in case something happens to me."

"Happens to you?" I repeat with my jaw gaping. "Like what?"

"Sometimes the MC makes enemies..."

Enemies?

"Like you could get shot?" I ask, and then a memory from the year before hits me. "The pregnant woman?"

Warren nods his head solemnly. "That was the president's wife."

"And you...you look out for the president?"

"Yes."

"Jesus, Warren!" I exclaim. "Why would you want to be a part of something that could get you killed?"

"Because it's more than that," he answers. "I know it sounds bad and has the potential to be dangerous, but it's also a brotherhood. The guys there are like my second family. I have their backs and they have mine, no matter what." While he's talking, he starts absently rubbing at his forearm, and after a moment, I notice the long, jagged scar his fingers are tracing.

"That wasn't a work injury, was it?" I accuse, pointing at the mark on his arm. I remember seeing him while it was still red and inflamed, and him waving off my questions, claiming it was no big deal.

"It was sort of a work injury," he hedges as he jerks his hand away from the scar.

"Warren!" Both Nova and I draw his name out in a warning tone.

"All right, all right. A guy was going to stab Torin, and I blocked the knife. Well, sort of blocked it, by getting stabbed in the arm. It really wasn't a big deal, though," he adds under his breath.

I shake my head as I let that information sink in. "And Maddox is about to become a member."

"He is." Then he asks, "Why?"

"Just wondering."

"He was good to you that week, right?"

"Yes!" I exclaim, because he's asked me half a dozen times already. "He was a perfect gentleman." *He always made sure I came first.*

"Listen, Audrey, I didn't tell you about the MC because I didn't want you to think...less of me."

"Less of you? Why would I think less of you?" I ask in confusion.

"Well, if I'm being honest with you and myself, not everything the club does is one hundred percent legal. And right now...well, it's probably best that I'm telling you all of this now, because the federal government has us under their thumb."

"Oh shit," I mutter in concern. "Like, you could get arrested?"

He looks to Nova sadly before he says, "It's a possibility. And if anything happens to me, I would hate to put the burden on you, but you're Ren's godmother."

Understanding exactly what he means, I tell him, "Of course I would take care of Ren!"

"I know you would. Let's hope it doesn't come to that."

"Is this, the MC, the reason Ren got taken away?" I ask.

"Yes."

Looking to Nova, who I know was his social worker because she called and questioned me, I start to open my mouth and say something not nice, when Warren speaks up. "It wasn't her fault! Nova was just doing her job and she helped me get Ren back."

"If you say so," I grumble, crossing my arms over my chest.

"That's all behind us now," Warren says when he takes Nova's hand in his. "We just have to wait and see what happens with the feds and have plans in place for the worst-case scenario."

"I don't like that you kept all of this from me," I tell him.

"I was just trying to keep you and Ren safe while doing the best I could to put food on the table and keep a roof over our heads," he says. "If I thought there was a better way, I wouldn't have joined the MC. Now, though, I wouldn't leave them if I could. They're my brothers and I'm gonna stick by them through thick and thin."

"Are you sure it's the best place for a guy like Maddox?" I ask in concern.

"No," Warren replies. "And that's why we've waited so long before voting him in, hoping he would change his mind before he commits to this lifestyle. But it's what he wants, so it looks like it's going to finally happen."

Being in town, knowing I'm so close to Maddox, makes me want to see him again, and maybe try to talk him out of joining the Savage Kings. If only I knew where to find him.

"Wait," I say when a thought hits me. "Do the Savage Kings own the Savage Asylum bar?"

"Yeah, why?" War asks.

"No reason," I tell him before I get to my feet. "Would you mind watching over Stella for a little while? I want to catch up with some friends from high school who are home for the summer break."

"Sure," Warren agrees. "Nova and I are having a movie night with Ren. You can join us when you get back."

"Sounds good," I tell him.

CHAPTER ELEVEN

Maddox

"IF A MEMBER ASKS FOR ANY FUCKING THING, YOU GET YOUR ASS moving in a hurry," I explain to our two new prospects. "If one of them calls you in the middle of the night, you sleep with the burner phone in your bed and answer it on the first ring. If one of them asks you to move a dead body, you don't even ask for a shovel. They'll either give you one or you'll be expected to dig the grave with your own two—"

"You're joking, right?" Mike asks me.

"If a member is speaking," I say, raising my voice as I glare at him, "you never fucking interrupt!"

"Jeez. Sorry," he mutters. "But it's impossible for me to tell when you're serious and when you're fucking with us."

"How about this, if I'm not laughing, I'm not fucking with you. Understood?"

"Yes, sir," both guys reply to me.

I have to admit, I could really get used to this being in charge shit.

It's nice not to be the lowest member on the totem pole. Soon, I'll even have my patches...

Sunlight spills into the dimly-lit bar, and I'm not sure why but as crazy as it sounds, I know it's Audrey before I even turn around and see her. I could just feel her close proximity, like she's a magnetic force I can't resist, even if I wanted to.

Without another word to our prospects, I head straight for her. The smile on her face when she sees me is brighter than any beacon from a lighthouse. Still, I can't help but ask, "What the hell are you doing here?" when she throws her arms around my neck.

Shit.

I quickly glance around to make sure War's not in the bar before I hug her back, trying not to think about how good it feels to have her in my arms again.

Pulling away from her before I do something stupid, like kiss her or fuck her on the bar, I ask, "I mean, is everything okay?" trying to make amends for my first question that came out too harsh.

"It's good to see you too," Audrey replies sarcastically with a smirk. "I just talked to War..."

"You told him about us?" I hiss.

"No, not about that," she says with a roll of her dark brown eyes. "I asked him about the MC and he told me the truth. *Finally.* Anyway, I was in town and I wanted to see you."

"You shouldn't be here," I warn her. "If he comes by—"

"He won't be by," she assures me. "At least, not for a while."

"How do you know that?" I ask.

"Because I just walked in on him and his woman getting busy. And then he'll be going to pick up Ren from daycare soon."

"Oh," I mutter, figuring that means he's made up with Nova. But I'm still not sure what Audrey's doing in the bar.

"So, why are you here?" I ask. "In the Savage Asylum? Someone could tell War."

"I'm pretty sure that no one here knows who I am since I didn't even know about the MC until you told me about them. And, well, I wanted to see you again," she says, reaching up to pinch the sides of my cut between her finger and thumb to tug me a little closer. "Maybe kiss you and...more?"

More? Fuck yes, I want more.

Shit, I'm supposed to be showing the prospects the ropes. I glance over at the two guys, who are watching me, and then back to Audrey, who looks so damn sexy in her short summer dress and strappy fuck-me heels. Her cheeks are flushed from the heat, reminding me of how they flushed for me during our three days and nights together. Fuck, that was good, and I've missed her like crazy every second since I walked out her door.

But War would murder me...

"Is this a bad time?" Audrey asks in concern.

"I'm, ah, sort of on babysitting duty right now," I explain to her.

"Should I go?" she asks. "Or are they old enough to watch?"

I choke out a laugh. "You're kidding, right?"

"No," she replies, looking up at me, innocently blinking those big chocolate eyes. "They look like they're over eighteen."

"Are you trying to get me killed?" I whisper to her. "Because that's what your brother will do to me if he finds out about the other week or today."

"So, there's going to be a today?" she asks cheerfully.

"I didn't say that," I reply.

"Do you want me to leave?"

"No," I answer without any hesitation. "Just give me a second to think. It's really hard to do that when you're standing right in front of me, wearing a dress that I could so easily bend you over and fuck you in."

"Oh yeah, let's do that," Audrey suggests, pinching my T-shirt in her fingers and grazing my lower abs, which doesn't help my strategic thought process at all.

"Prospects," I say. "Go...go clean the kitchen!"

"What?" Mike asks, but thankfully, Cedric gives him a push toward the back to get him heading that way.

"Ooh, will they do anything you tell them to?" Audrey asks. "Because I will too."

"You really are trying to kill me," I tell her before I grab her hand and tug her out through the bar door and around the side of the building. There's never any foot traffic through here so we should have a few moments of privacy. Which is apparently going to be all the time it takes for me to erupt since Audrey only lets me press her into the wall and kiss her lips for a few seconds before she falls to her knees. I worry about the rough pavement causing abrasions on her soft skin but before I can pull her up, she's unzipping my jeans and pulling out my cock. And I need her so fucking badly my entire body is trembling.

Audrey's mouth opens wide as she looks up at me and then wraps her lips around half my cock.

"Jesus Christ, woman," I groan when she pulls off and then surges forward again, causing even more of my rock-hard flesh to disappear into her hot, wet mouth.

Needing a distraction to keep from blowing my load when her head starts to bob faster and faster, I busy my shaky hands with pulling out my wallet from the back pocket of my jeans to hunt for the condom I stashed in there. I toss the leather down on the ground and let Audrey suck me three more wonderful times before I reluctantly step back to remove myself from her mouth.

"Wanna be inside of you," I tell her as I rip the condom wrapper open with my teeth and then roll the rubber up my damp shaft. Incapable of full sentences, I also mutter, "Up."

Audrey stands, then reaches down to pull her white panties free from her shoes and holds them up in offering.

"Thanks," I tell her, as I snatch them from her hand with a grin and shove them into the pocket of my cut.

I reach for her hips as I lean down and slant my lips over hers, kissing her deeply while I lower a hand to cup her between her thighs. My tongue slips between her parted lips at the same time my fingers part her lower ones.

"God, you're so fucking wet," I whisper.

"I missed you," Audrey says before we're too busy attacking each other to speak. Her fingers are tugging on my hair while mine are playing with her clit and sinking inside of her tight pussy.

"Fuck me," she eventually says. "I want to come on your cock."

"God, yes," I groan as I remove my hand and spin her around so that she's facing the building, her palms flattened against it.

Glancing each way, I make sure there's no one lurking around before I hike up her skirt and then line my cock up to push my way slowly inside of her body. Both of us moan at the amazing sensation of me filling her up until I'm as deep as I can go. I stay buried there for a few moments to revel in the way we fit together so perfectly, like she was made for me.

And also, to try and talk my dick down from jack-hammering into her just to get myself off before Audrey's even close.

"Maddox?" Audrey asks while squirming on my cock to try and make me move.

"Yeah, baby?" I reply as I place my lips on the side of her neck.

"Move."

"Move?" I repeat, teasing her.

"Yes, move!" she demands, bucking her hips to try and fuck me. But I flatten her much smaller body to the bricks and lace my fingers with her splayed ones while invading every inch of her.

"You're not the one in control here," I remind her. "I'll move when I damn well want to."

When she whimpers and says, "Please?" I finally give in. I withdraw my hips just a little before slamming them forward again.

"Oh my god," Audrey moans. "Again? Please?"

Just hearing her beg makes my cock throb.

"Only because you asked nicely," I tell her before I start to fuck her with small, shallow strokes. Gradually, I speed up a little more and slam inside of her harder until the two of us are both incapable of anything other than broken sobs, begging for relief.

"Come on, baby," I plead while reaching around Audrey's body and finding her swollen, needy clit that I rub with the pad of my finger. "Give it to me. I know you're close."

"Yes," she cries out. "So close. *Uhh, Maddox!*"

I'm not sure if anything has ever felt as good as finally letting go, giving myself over to the pleasure and riding the waves with Audrey. Her moans and cries have me coming so hard the world goes dark again for a few incredible seconds.

Then I blink, and the sun is shining down on us in the Savage Asylum alley, and I realize just how stupid and selfish I've been to let myself bring War's sister out here and fuck her where someone could've seen us.

Audrey's a good girl, even if she does have a wild streak. She deserves better than getting fucked here where some guys take pisses and toss their cigarettes.

"I probably need to get back inside," I tell her, as I pull out of her and quickly remove the condom.

"And you want me to leave," she says in understanding.

"I'm supposed to be watching the prospects, and if your brother found out..."

"No, I get it," Audrey says when she turns around and puts her dress back in place while I zip up. "I got what I came for."

"I love seeing you and...and being with you," I tell her, reaching up to brush her long hair behind her shoulder. "But I can't keep doing this. There's a lot on the line..." *Like my head.*

"Yeah, you're pulling the plug. I get it," she agrees on a sigh. Then she stands on her tippy-toes to kiss my cheek. "See ya, Maddox."

And without another word, Audrey walks away from me, like it was way too easy.

CHAPTER TWELVE

Maddox

I KNOW I'M IN TROUBLE AS SOON AS I WALK BACK INTO THE clubhouse...and Reece is sitting at the bar with the two prospects. He rarely comes up here unless he's hanging out with some of the guys, and right now, the veins in his arms and neck are bulging like he really wants to hit me.

"I found one of your prospects downstairs and came up to return him to you," Reece grits out between his clenched teeth. "Check his phone."

"Shit," I mutter as I glance at the two guys, who both look nervous. "Which one?"

"Does it matter?" Reece huffs.

"Hand them over," I say with my palm out, waiting for their devices. Cedric offers his first, followed slowly by Mike.

"Mad Dog and I need to have a talk. You two keep your asses glued on these chairs." Reece then points to one of the cameras with a red glowing dot in the corner of the room. "I'll know if you squirm even an inch!" he warns them.

Fuck. This is bad. Reece is always in a grumpy mood but today, he is livid.

Phones in hand, I follow him to the keypad and watch as he punches in a new code. "If you let them see you punch in the numbers again, I'll take your fingers off," he grumbles over his shoulder.

"How do you know they got the code from watching me?" I ask as I jog down the steps behind him. "I haven't even been down here since I was given the prospects."

"Keen observation," he says, without looking back at me. "But that means you still let them get close enough to see one of our brothers enter the code."

"Fuck," I mutter under my breath as we head inside his apartment. As soon as I'm inside, he gets in my face and slams the door behind me.

"What the fuck were you thinking?" he snarls.

"Fine. I heard you loud and clear!" I reply. "I won't let the prospects near the keypad. But it's not like there's anything secretive going on down here..."

"No, but there's sure as fuck something *secretive* going on upstairs. In the alley, to be exact."

"Oh."

I slip the two prospects' phones into my jeans pocket when I realize what this chewing out is really about.

"You're fucking War's sister!" Reece asks. "Are you planning to follow in your father's footsteps and die young too?"

"Wait," I say, holding up my palm in confusion. "First of all, how did you know what I was doing outside, and how do you know she's War's sister?"

"Cameras!" he exclaims, pointing over to the many, many screens around the room that show various parts of the building...and outside of it.

"Shit," I groan, while scrubbing a hand down my embarrassed face before the indignation hits. "Hold up. You were *watching* us?"

"It's my job to keep an eye out for threats!" he yells. "It's not my fault that you picked the wrong place to fuck the wrong girl instead of babysitting the fucking prospects, like you were told to do!"

"Fine, it was stupid of me to do that outside with her, but I told the prospects to clean the kitchen and I wasn't gone long."

"Yeah, I'm well aware of that too," he responds snidely as he crosses his arms over his chest.

Instead of arguing that I made sure she still came, I ask, "You still haven't said how you know she's War's sister."

"I ran her license plate. The car's in his name," he grumbles. "Everyone thinks I'm a genius, when all I do is run a few numbers through a database and *ta-da*, I get answers."

"Oh," I reply. "So, are you going to tell War?"

"Are you?" he counters.

"No."

"Why not?" Reece asks.

"Because he would kill me."

"Good. So, you're not as dumb as you look," he scoffs before he goes over and sits down in his Captain Kirk-looking computer chair.

"Can I go now?" I ask. "Are we done talking about this?"

"We're done talking about your premature ejaculation, but not the prospects."

"There was no premature ejaculation!" I yell defensively. "It was fucking amazing sex, for me *and* her! Something you wouldn't know anything about. People living in glass basements really shouldn't be throwing stones, should they?"

Rather than be offended by my remark, Reece only smirks and shakes his head.

"Go through the phones, and then get the hell out of my apartment," he says.

"You were serious about that?" I ask as I pull them out. "I thought you were just fucking with them."

"No," he says with a sigh. "The dumbass really was wandering around down here with his phone out. I thought I would let you do the honors."

"Should we cut him loose for that?" I ask.

"What do you think?" Reece asks.

Shrugging, I say, "Maybe he was just curious. I wouldn't know, since I lived down here for two years before I became a prospect."

"Yes," he agrees. "But did you ever step foot in the chapel without permission?"

"He was in the chapel?" I ask.

"Yep."

"Shit."

"Check his photos," Reece suggests, so I do.

"Wow. The stupid fucker took pics of the table," I tell him, turning the screen around to show him.

"Why would he do that?" Reece asks, not like he doesn't know the answer, but wants me to come up with my own.

"To post and brag about on social media?" I suggest.

"Maybe. Kids today do like to share photos of every fucking thing," Reece grumbles. "Keep looking."

I pull up the calls and text chats next.

"Hmm," I say, as I go through a chat log.

"What?" Reece asks.

"Mike has been talking to someone on a chat log named only as *PB*," I tell him. "That's odd, right? No one goes by the initials P.B., do they?"

"Not that I've ever heard," Reece agrees. "What do they talk about?"

"Mostly Mike is just checking in, saying 'No news today. I'll call if something comes up.'"

"When did the log start?" he asks.

I scroll up to the top to get to the first message. "A few weeks ago."

"The exact date?" Reece demands.

"August sixth."

"And what was August sixth?" he asks me.

"I dunno. The beginning of the month?"

"You really should keep better records of shit," he huffs. "It was the day we picked our potential new prospects."

"So, you think that's significant?"

"Maybe not normally," he replies. "But when the feds are trying to get their hooks in the Kings, hell yes."

"Holy shit!" I exclaim in understanding. "You think he's a snitch? But we vetted him!"

"Do you think he's a snitch?" he asks.

"Jesus," I mutter. "It's starting to look like it's a possibility."

"'Looks like a possibility' isn't having proof. We need *proof*," Reece explains. "Undisputable proof. How do you suggest we do that?"

"Follow him? Bug his phone?" I suggest. "Hell, I don't know. You're the expert on snooping on people."

"Only to keep my people safe," he argues. "And I think that, in this case, it may be time for us to try another method of investigation."

He swivels his chair to look at the screen showing the bar, where Mike and Cedric are still sitting as still as statues.

"If we let him leave now, after he knows we looked at his phone, he may not ever come back," I point out.

"Exactly," Reece agrees when he spins back around to look at me. "If we want answers from him, we're gonna have to extract them by force."

"Torture?" I ask in understanding.

"It only hurts if he doesn't talk," he says with an evil smile.

"You're looking forward to inflicting some pain on him, though, aren't you?"

"Hell yes, I am. When I find a roach, I squash that motherfucker," Reece replies. "But we can't do it here."

"Then where?" I ask before it hits me. A place the Kings own,

LANE HART & D.B. WEST

with no one around for miles, and so dirty that any evidence could easily be destroyed. "The salvage yard?"

"See, now you're thinking like a Savage King," he replies with a chuckle. Getting to his feet, he rubs his hands together like a comic villain and says, "Today, I'm actually looking forward to leaving the basement."

"But if you leave, who'll watch the cameras?" I ask.

Reece is already pulling out his phone and putting it to his ear. "Fast Eddie and I are gonna switch roles for a few hours."

...

Audrey

I DIDN'T TELL Maddox the real reason I was in town—that my former professor creeped me out in the produce section of the grocery store. In fact, we didn't really talk much at all. But I guess I can't blame him, since that's all I acted like I wanted, when really, I wanted a lot more.

Turns out, Maddox doesn't.

He said he's worried about my brother finding out about us, and I know he would probably get his ass kicked by Warren because he is so protective. If Maddox actually wanted to keep seeing me, then I think I could talk my brother down. Probably.

Anyway, I was most likely overreacting, and Professor Burrows was just all dirty talk and not being serious. He wouldn't have told anyone about the two of us being together last year, or he would be risking not only his job but his entire career, since he teaches at an all-girl Methodist university.

I decide I'll pack up my things and head back to campus tomorrow, since I feel like the fourth wheel here at Warren's house. Ren thinks Nova has been staying in my room when, in reality, she and Warren are shacking up, which makes me think things between them are pretty serious. My brother is incredibly protective over me and Ren, so if he's letting a woman stay in the house, he must love her and trust her not to up and leave, hurting himself and Ren.

Speaking of my adorable nephew... "Good night, sweet boy," I tell Ren before I kiss his forehead and tuck him in after his third bedtime book.

"Night, Audrey," he says, and then leans over his small bed to pet his new best friend. "Night, Stella."

Ren was so happy to see me, and then the kitten was an added bonus since he's never had a pet. Warren always said he was too busy to look after any animals too, and now I know why—living a double life must take up a lot of his time.

Thankfully, my brother has been in a really great mood since Nova is here with him, so he barely even lifted an eyebrow at my new pet visiting.

And while I'm happy that everything seems to be going great for my brother, that doesn't mean I've let him off the hook for lying to me for years.

Back in the living room, Warren and Nova have the volume down on the television, watching some medical sitcom when I join them.

"Ren finally let you escape?" Warren asks with a grin.

"He did. After three stories," I say as I plop down on the sofa, and Stella climbs up and jumps in my lap. I give her scruffy head a rub because she was so good playing with Ren and didn't scratch him, even when he picked her up and held her like a baby.

"I'm surprised he didn't try to abduct your cat for the night," he replies with a chuckle. "Now you're gonna have him wanting a pet."

"He should have a pet," I tell him while I keep rubbing mine. "Mom and Dad let us have pets..."

"Low blow," he grumbles.

He thinks *that's* low, when he lied to me for who knows how many years.

"Did you ever work as a mechanic in an auto shop?" I ask him.

"Yes," Warren answers. "But just before we left Texas. I never worked in one here."

"Wow," I scoff. "So, you've been lying to me for almost seven years, ever since we moved here from Texas?"

"I wouldn't call it lying," he replies. "It was more like withholding the entire truth."

"Same thing," I point out. "Do you carry a gun?"

"Yes."

"Have you ever shot anyone with it?"

"Maybe."

"Warren!" I exclaim, both at his half-answer and the fact that I think he has. "You shot someone?"

"Am I on trial here, or what?" he huffs. "It's bad enough that I have this one questioning me constantly," he says when he kisses Nova's nose.

"Do you approve of my brother's secret life?" I ask her.

"I'm not sure if I approve, but I'm trying to accept all of him, the good *and* the bad," she answers.

"So that's a no?"

"Don't put words in her mouth," Warren responds. "And the less you know about the MC, the better."

"What if I told you that about my life?" I challenge. "Don't worry about what happens at school. The less you know, the better."

"What is there to know about an all-girls university?" Warren asks. "You eat, sleep, and go to class. That's it, right?"

"Yeah, Warren, that's all there is," I say with a roll of my eyes. He has no clue what it's like to be a woman at the mercy of the men of the world.

And sure, I blame myself for the position I'm in with Professor Burrows, since I'm the one who first came on to him. But then he blackmailed me for sex for weeks because he could, and there was nothing I could do to stop him unless I want to drop out of school. No one would believe me over him anyway, not when he puts all the blame at my feet and says I seduced him. While that's true, I didn't intend to fall into a trap where I had to do him whenever he said until the end of the semester.

I don't think I can handle that again, if what he said about Professor Talbot is true. But I need the class to graduate and it's only taught in the fall semester by one freaking man!

When the semester starts, I'll just sit in the back of the class, keep my head down, and study my ass off to make sure I pass. I won't even smile at the man on the chance he'll get the wrong idea. I'm sure that I'm just overreacting, and everything will be fine.

CHAPTER THIRTEEN

Maddox

"You can't do this to me!" Mike yells at us, as Sax and I hold him down on the wooden chair and Reece ties his ankles to the legs and his hands through the slats behind his back.

"I think we just did," Reece remarks before he comes around and stands in front of him. "Let him go, he's not going anywhere," he tells me.

I release my hold on his shoulders and heave a sigh of relief that this part is over. Sweat is dripping down my forehead and neck because dragging the asshole from the clubhouse to the salvage yard's old garage, then holding him down while restraining him was hard work.

The big room is empty, except for oil and grease stains. The stale, automotive smell reminds me of my time training, also known as Reece whipping me into ass-kicking shape.

"Now," Reece starts, "do you want to start talking, or do you want us to find new and creative ways to hurt you until you decide to talk?"

"Talk?" Mike asks. "I don't know what you're talking about."

"Who is the contact PB in your phone?" Reece asks.

Yeah, we could've called the number to see who answers, but if we used Mike's phone and didn't say anything, they would worry he's in trouble. And if we use another phone, even a burner, and then something unfortunate happens to Mike, it could come back on us. So, Reece is determined to make the man talk instead.

"Peanut Butter," Mike answers. "He's a friend of Jelly. Maybe you know him?"

"Hit him in his smart mouth for us, Maddox," Sax instructs. I gladly haul my fist back and slam it into his mouth so hard his teeth cut his lips open and blood drips from them.

"We're not playing games here, son." Reece kneels down in front of Mike. "You want to try and be funny again, or do you want to start explaining who you've been texting since you got your prospect cut. You give us some answers, maybe we'll let you walk out of here alive."

"I'm not scared of you," Mike says. He's clearly an idiot who doesn't know Reece like I do.

"Tool time?" Sax asks Reece.

"Maddox, go get them from the van," Reece says, tipping his head toward the door. I head out and grab his toolbox from the van, curious to see what's inside.

Before I pick up the oversized toolbox, I flip the tabs to open it up to see what implements Reece has packed. I'm not sure if I'm disappointed or relieved when I give the tools a quick shuffle, revealing only mundane pliers, wrenches, and clamps. Other than the propane blowtorch, none of it looks particularly intimidating.

When I get back to the room where Mike is being restrained, I set the toolbox on a table and then step away as Reece comes over and flips open the lid.

"All right, gentlemen, let's get to work," Reece says. Turning back to Mike, he asks conversationally, "You ever seen that show on HBO, *Game of Thrones*?"

I haven't seen the show, but for some reason, the comment causes Mike to start trembling violently. He takes a deep breath to steady himself, then says, "Yeah, I've seen it. Read the books too."

"Oh shit, look at this literate motherfucker!" Reece laughs. "That's good, that's really good. You've got some idea then, of the things I can do to you. Things that won't kill you, but will make you... different. Some might even say, unrecognizable. Now, are you sure you don't have anything you want to tell me before we get started?" As Reece was talking, I watched him slip a pair of needle-nosed pliers into the back pocket of his jeans, before walking to stand behind Mike's chair.

Mike hangs his head but doesn't say anything in reply as Reece crouches down behind him. "All right, then. Time to get medieval and all that. We'll start by destroying things that might grow back, if you live long enough."

I can't see what Reece is doing behind the chair where Mike's hands are tied, but I think I understand when his head suddenly jerks up and he lets out a long gargling scream. Sure enough, Reece pops up holding the pliers, with one ragged fingernail gripped tightly at the tip.

"You say something, champ?" Reece asks when Mike's scream dissolves into a gasping sob. "Anything at all you want to get off your chest?" he asks again, dropping the fingernail on Mike's lap. "No? Ok then, back to work I go. Remember now, you can stop me anytime," he adds as he crouches behind the chair.

I have seen some shit in my life, but the next few minutes of watching Reece work on Mike will be burned in my memory forever. He works methodically, and every few seconds, another fingernail joins the growing pile on Mike's lap. After what seems like an eternity but could only have been a couple of minutes, Reece stands up and walks around the front of the chair, then sits down cross-legged in front of his victim.

"All done back there!" he says cheerfully, pulling a shop rag out of his pocket to wipe his pliers. "You sure you don't want to tell me more about your friend 'Peanut Butter' before I start working on these little piggies down here?"

Mike is still conscious, gasping and wheezing as Reece begins untying his boots. It takes him a minute to get them off of Mike since he's tied so tightly to the chair. "Still holding out on me? All right then." Reece chuckles, bending down to begin working on the feet.

I look over to Sax, who I notice is looking pale as his trembling hands light a cigarette. "You mind if I get one of those from you?" I ask him.

"Didn't know you smoked," he says, as he passes me the pack of Marlboros and his lighter.

"I don't," I reply grimly. "Shit like this will make a man want to start."

"Shit like this will drive a man fucking insane." Sax shudders. "That boy screams like a wildcat getting fucked with a drill."

"Don't give Reece any ideas," I mutter.

We both walk away as we smoke, circling back around once we've thrown the butts out into the yard. By that time, Reece is back over at his toolbox, cleaning his pliers, and Mike is slumped over, noisily sobbing into his own lap.

"Think I almost had him," Reece idly comments as we approach.

"Yeah? What did he finally say?" I ask him.

"He started muttering that we'll kill him if he tells us, he knows we will. I tried to reassure him, and told him I would eventually kill him anyway, but I think he started passing out. Sax, go run a bucket of water from the hose outside and dump it on him. Let's perk him up and see if he's ready to give this up."

"Ok," Sax agrees, jogging outside.

"What could he have done that's so bad he thinks we'll kill him over it?" I wonder aloud.

"That's the meat of it, isn't it?" Reece replies. "He obviously thinks he's done something so terrible it's worth all this, or maybe he's protecting something. Either way, Phase Two will loosen his lips. No one gets past Phase Two."

"Do I even want to know what 'Phase Two' is?" I ask with a raised eyebrow.

"You never want to find out, no." Reece sighs. "Looks like we might not have a choice, though."

Sax returns, lugging a five-gallon bucket, sloshing over with water. He walks up behind Mike and unceremoniously dumps the entire thing over him, drawing another horrified screech from the traitorous prospect.

"Shut up," Reece barks at him. "You're fine, you fucking pussy." Walking over to him, he slaps Mike gently on both cheeks, then grabs him by the chin to jerk his head up. "You ready to talk now, or do you want this to keep going?"

"I can't." Mike gasps. "You're going to kill me. It dies with me, it'll be over. Just get on with it."

"Now that's a bad attitude to have," Reece says as he scrubs a hand through Mike's damp hair. "I told you before you can get out of this alive if you just cooperate with me. Come on, spit it out and let's put all this behind us, Mike."

"I told you, I can't. I know you're full of shit. If I tell you anything, I'm dead. Do whatever you have to do."

Reece sighs, his expression looking, for all the world, like a father disappointed in an unruly child. "All right, then. For the next phase, we're going to take care of those wounds on your hands and feet. We don't want them becoming infected, so we're going to go ahead and cauterize them."

"What?" Mike gasps, which is exactly how I feel.

Reece digs in his toolbox and brings out the propane torch, twisting the valve and then clicking the trigger. He makes a great show of adjusting the flame as he walks back to Mike, then once again crouches down in front of him. "You sure about this, kid?" Reece whispers.

Mike just hangs his head, refusing to make eye contact with him. Before Reece can begin, I turn my back, digging another cigarette out of Sax's pack.

"Good idea," Sax whispers beside me as the screams begin from behind us. "Want to head out into the yard?"

"Yeah, man, let's...let's give them some space," I say shakily, as the first whiff of burning meat washes over us.

Once we're outside, Sax takes a deep drag on his cigarette and says, "This ain't my favorite part of this gig, you know."

"None of us like it," I agree, "but he's done something, and if he ratted us out somehow to the feds, well...this is what happens to rats."

"I hope he is a rat," Sax says fiercely. "I hope to god he is, so...so I can justify all this. We've all got secrets, man, things we don't want people to know. I hope he's not trying to hide something stupid, and he really did something worth all this."

"That's a weird way to look at it, but yeah, I get it," I reply. Shit, how much torture would I take to keep my secret with Audrey away from War? Should I even keep it a secret? God, I wish I had a reason to see her, any reason that didn't make me look like a pussy-whipped bitch.

"You say something?" Sax asks me.

"Huh?" I cough, choking on the cigarette smoke. "Shit, sorry, man, just talking to myself."

"Thought I heard you say 'pussy-whipped bitch.'" Sax laughs. "That is what he sounds like in there, isn't it?"

I nod in agreement, not wanting to tell him that no, it's what I feel like, out here. We both light up another cigarette and stay outside, until Reece steps out and joins us a few minutes later. Uncharacteristically, he lights up a smoke too, and stands there with us in silence for a moment.

"All right," Reece finally huffs. "We're done for the night."

"We are?" I ask.

"For today, right? Doesn't sound like he told you anything," Sax says.

"Seriously?" I ask. "He still hasn't told you shit?"

"We're going to try another approach. We'll leave him here for a few days without food and water. Eventually, he'll crack when the choice is talk or die," Reece replies.

"Days?" I repeat.

"Yeah, days, son," Reece says. "Hunger and thirst can break a man when nothing else will. You're on first watch. Make sure he doesn't leave. That's your one and only job until we come back."

"Okay," I agree.

Looks like I won't be getting any sleep tonight.

CHAPTER FOURTEEN

Audrey

THE FIRST DAY OF MY FALL CLASSES IS GOING GREAT...UNTIL Organic Chemistry with Professor Talbot. It's obvious, by the way the silver fox stands a little too close and laughs a little too much with students who come up and talk to him, that he thinks he's God's gift to women.

Just like Professor Burrows.

"Miss O'Neil, I need to see you after class," Professor Talbot says, as everyone starts putting their things away in their backpacks.

While I wish I could say I'm surprised that he's called me out, I sort of assumed it was only a matter of time, based on my grocery store conversation with Professor Burrows.

My heartbeat is hammering away at an unhealthy pace as I quickly pack up and head down the auditorium stairs, wanting to have this conversation while other students are still milling about.

"Yes, sir?" I ask when I get to his podium.

"It's nice to meet you, Audrey. I look forward to a wonderful semester," he says, holding his hand out for me to take it.

"You too," I reply politely as I put my hand in his to shake. He doesn't let go right away.

"I've been told that science isn't your favorite subject," he says with a grin. "Such a shame."

"No, sir, it's not, but I plan to study and work very hard this semester."

"I'm also aware of your...unique but highly effective study techniques from last semester," he replies. "The *hard* work you put into Professor Burrows' Physics class was impressive."

And here we go.

"I would prefer to stick to the traditional methods of studying this year," I tell him, trying to shoot down his implication.

"It would be a shame for you to struggle through the semester and come up short at the end of the year, Miss O'Neil. Failing would mean having to postpone your graduation another year. That would be a real shame. Better to get ahead of the curve now, don't you think?"

He's going to fail me if I don't sleep with him. That's basically what he's saying.

Leaning closer to whisper in my ear, since there are still a handful of students in the auditorium, he says, "I'll see you at Burrows' house tonight, eight sharp. Don't keep us waiting. It's going to be an enlightening encounter that you'll never forget."

"No, thanks," I respond before I start to walk away. He claps a hand down on my elbow and squeezes it, stopping me.

"Then I'll see you next year in Organic Chemistry, and the year after that, and so on, Miss O'Neil," he threatens through clenched teeth before he eventually lets me go.

I rush out of the auditorium and practically run back to my apartment across campus.

By the time I get inside, my breaths are infrequent, coming in partial gasps.

I recognize the tightness in my chest and the trembling as a panic attack. Usually it's thunderstorms that cause them.

I'm starting to realize there's something I'm even more terrified of than lightning, and I have no idea what I'm going to do about it.

CHAPTER FIFTEEN

Maddox

"Hey, he's still here!" Sax says when he comes into the old salvage yard garage the next afternoon. His voice sounds loud, echoing around the room that was silent after Mike had stopped crying and bitching for a few hours to get some sleep. He's awake now.

"Water," Mike croaks when Sax approaches him.

"I'll think about it," Sax says to him.

"Really?" Mike asks.

"No," Sax responds with a slap of his palm to his face. "Not unless you start talking."

Mike's head hangs in defeat, so Sax comes over to where I've been sitting on the hard cement floor for so long, I can't feel my ass or my legs.

"You did good. Now go get some sleep," Sax says, offering me a hand up so I can get to my numb feet.

"Thanks," I tell him before I head outside. Realizing that Sax and Reece took the van back to the clubhouse and Sax rode his bike over today, I start walking the mile back, ready to crash into bed and sleep for the next twelve hours.

I don't even make it downstairs before Cedric stops me at the bar.

"Hey, Maddox. Got a second?"

"Not now," I tell him. "After I sleep."

"Okay, but she said it can't wait."

"She?" I repeat in confusion. "She who?"

"The girl that just called the bar, looking for you. She said it's important and that you didn't have her number, but you know where she lives…"

"Shit," I mutter. It has to be Audrey. Glancing around the bar to make sure there are no brothers around, I ask, "Did she leave her name, by chance?"

"Yeah," he says, wetting his lips nervously. "Her name was Stella."

"Stella?"

"I'm certain that's what she said. I wrote it down and the number from caller ID," he says, pulling out a piece of paper from his pocket and holding it up to me. "I didn't know where you were, and Reece knew but wouldn't tell me, so I tried to call you on your cell phone and it went straight to voicemail."

"Fuck, my phone must be dead again." I yank the paper out of his hand. "Thanks, Cedric. You did good," I tell him, repeating Sax's encouraging words.

Going around behind the bar, I pick up the landline and dial the number on the piece of paper for "Stella."

"Hello?" I don't get the cat, instead Audrey answers.

"Hey, it's me," I say.

"Maddox! I'm so sorry to call but I didn't know what to do, and I can't tell Warren…"

"Can't tell him what?" I ask. "Is everything okay?"

"No," she replies with a sniffle and I realize that she's been crying. "Can you come over?"

"You want me to come over? To Wilmington? Right now?" I ask, since it's not just down the road but over an hour away.

"Please?"

I haven't had any sleep and I'm dead tired, still I find myself saying, "I'm on my way."

"Thanks, Maddox," she responds before hanging up.

Going over to Cedric, I tell him, "I need to take the club's van for a few hours to run an errand. I'll charge my phone on the road and have it ready if anyone needs me."

"Okay," he replies, then asks, "Where's Mike? I haven't seen him in a while."

"No clue," I lie before I walk out of the Savage Asylum.

...

WHEN AUDREY OPENS the apartment door an hour later, she looks even worse than she sounded on the phone. Her eyes are red and puffy, and she's distraught, appearing as if her world is coming apart.

"What's going on? Are you okay?" I ask as I wrap her in my arms and pull her to me.

"It's...it's a long story," she says. "And I don't know what I'm going to do."

"Come on," I tell her, taking her hand and leading her to the sofa, where I sit down and then pull her onto my lap. "How about you start from the beginning?"

"Okay," she agrees with a nod. "You remember that professor I told you about?"

"The one you slept with?" I ask.

"Yes."

"What about him?"

"I ran into him at the grocery store the other day, right before the semester started," she explains.

"What happened?" I ask, as dread as heavy as an anchor sinks in the pit of my stomach. Audrey and I may have been together only briefly, but I don't like thinking about her with another man. "Did you sleep with him again?"

"No," she answers, which is a relief for whatever reason. "But he mentioned that he's close friends with the professor I have this semester for Organic Chemistry."

"Yeah?"

"And that he had told him about us, what we did together," she explains. "He said that Professor Talbot was 'looking forward to meeting me.'"

"Okay," I reply, unsure why that would upset her this badly.

"Today, after class, Professor Talbot called me out to talk."

"What did he say?" I ask, even though I'm starting to get an idea.

"H-he basically told me I have to come over to Professor Burrows house tonight, or he would fail me over and over again," she says before she starts to sob against my chest.

Even then, it takes a few seconds for me to put everything together.

"He wants you to fuck him?" I exclaim.

Audrey nods her head and says, "And Professor Burrows."

"No," I tell her. "That's not going to happen!"

"What else can I do?" she cries. "I have to have this class to graduate, and if I try to transfer, Warren will get mad and want to know why..."

"You don't want to tell War about the professors because he would kill them," I reply with full understanding.

"Yes."

And Warren would, the consequences be damned. He's so protective of his family that he keeps his son and sister away from the MC, his brothers I know he loves. If he found out that someone was trying to manipulate Audrey, he would put a bullet through their heads.

That's when it all clicks into place—why Audrey called me instead and asked me to come over. She wants me to figure out what she should do. She's trusting *me* to help her without committing murder.

And fuck, having someone put that type of confidence in me for the first time sends a rush of adrenaline through my veins.

Even after all of the years in the MC, the crazy and illegal shit they've made me do, none of it was even half as important as making sure that some pervy-ass fucking professors never lay another finger on Audrey again.

"It's gonna be okay," I promise her, as I brush her hair back from her face and hold her to me. Because it will be. I'm going to make damn sure of that.

"You don't ever have to do anything you don't want to do. Got it?" I ask her. "I'll make sure neither of them ever looks at you again with a foul thought in their heads."

Audrey's head pops up and she wipes the tears on her cheeks before she asks nervously, "Wh-what are you going to do?"

"I won't kill them," I assure her, but that's all that I can guarantee. "But I'll teach them a lesson they won't forget. Does that work? Will you trust me on this?"

"Yes," she answers with a nod.

"What time were you supposed to go over tonight?"

"Eight."

"And you have the address?" I ask.

She nods again. "Yes."

"Good, so we just have to wait a little while," I say with a heavy exhale. My adrenaline is rushing, raring to go right now.

"Can I come too?" Audrey asks.

"Yeah, you can come," I agree. Having her there may be the only thing that stops me from killing the bastards.

And of course, it will be a lot easier to get them to open the door when they see her.

CHAPTER SIXTEEN

Audrey

SOMEHOW, I KNEW THAT MADDOX WOULD COME TO MY RESCUE, even though he's made it clear the two of us are done. Well, can you be done if you never started anything? We slept together for three days, and then once again at the MC's clubhouse, so that's all it ever was. Still, I think of him as a friend now. Maybe my only friend, who I can count on in times like this, when I find myself standing on the porch of a big, beautiful brick home, ringing the doorbell.

The heavy door opens and on the other side stands the man I once thought was handsome and sophisticated. Turns out, he was just an asshole who preyed on his students.

"I told Danny you would show," Professor Burrows says, wearing his typical uniform of a sweater vest and slacks. I bet he even wears his fancy brown dress shoes around his house all the time. Even though we fucked around together for weeks, he told me repeatedly he didn't want me to call him by his first name—Peter—even during sex. "Come on in. *Professor Talbot* is already here."

"Okay, but I brought a friend. I hope that's not a problem," I say with my hands clasped behind the back of my summer dress, trying to look the part of the innocent school girl.

"The more the merrier, as long as she can be discreet," he agrees. "Where's this friend of yours? Is she waiting in the car?" he asks before he takes a step out onto the porch.

"No, *he* is right fucking here," Maddox says when he jumps out of the bushes and shoves Professor Burrows' chest, knocking him back into the house so hard, he falls on his ass. Once Maddox is inside too, I follow and shut the door behind us to make sure no neighbors see what's going on.

The door barely clicks shut before Maddox falls on top of Professor Burrows and starts slamming his fists into his face while calling him various profane names.

"Fight back, you worthless piece of shit!" Maddox says.

"She...she started it. I swear!" Peter cries out in defense.

"Oh yeah?" Maddox asks, pausing with his fist pulled back. "Well, I'm finishing it."

"What's going on—" Professor Talbot asks as he walks into the foyer and takes in the scene on the floor. "Oh shit," he mutters before he starts backpedaling, and then turns to run further into the house the way he came.

He doesn't get far because Maddox jumps up and chases after him.

Since Professor Burrows doesn't look like he'll be going anywhere for a while, I kneel beside him and pull his phone from his pocket to make sure he can't try to call anyone.

"Please, make him leave! Or call nine-one-one," he begs me, with a bleeding lip and head. "You wanted it..."

"How about I call the police and tell them you blackmailed me for weeks instead?" I ask, holding up the device threateningly. "What I did was stupid, but what you did was illegal! So, you're going to take your beating so that you can keep your job, even though you don't deserve to get off so easily."

With that, I get up to go find Maddox.

He has Professor Talbot up against a wall in the kitchen, plowing his fist into his flabby abdomen until he doubles over. On the way to the ground, Maddox slams his knee into his face, likely busting his nose because blood starts to spray everywhere.

And Jesus, he's so fucking hot.

My avenging angel, not the bleeding professor.

I've never seen someone so tough and badass. Knowing that Maddox is so angry and inflicting pain on them for trying to hurt me makes me love him even more.

Oh shit.

No, I didn't mean to use that word. I don't love Maddox. I barely know him!

He's just a really amazing guy who is sweet and hot as sin, but doesn't want to be with me...

"Let's go, fucker," Maddox says before he grabs the back of Professor Talbot's shirt, where he's down on his hands and knees, then literally drags him through the living room and to the foyer to join his friend.

"I want you two to listen to me very closely," Maddox says when he crouches down to see their faces better on the ground. "If either of you say a single sleazy word to Audrey, I'm gonna come back here. Best-case scenario? You never walk again. Worst? You never *breathe* again. Is that clear?"

"Yes," both men mutter.

"I couldn't hear you," Maddox says as he turns his ear to them. "Yes, what?"

"Yes, sir," they both grumble.

"That's better," Maddox replies as he stands and straightens. "Now, apologize to Audrey and tell her that you will *never* try to blackmail her again for sex, and that she *is* going to pass this semester with flying fucking colors."

"I'm sorry," Professor Burrows says.

"I'm sorry. You don't have to come to my class. I-I'll pass you," Professor Talbot frantically tells me.

"No, I'm going to come to class and I'm going to earn whatever grade I get, fair and square," I tell him. "But I'm going to do it without touching either of you again."

Maddox holds out his palm for me. "Ready?"

"Ready," I agree, then throw Professor Burrows' phone at him before he leads me out the door.

"Thank you," I tell Maddox as we walk to my car, my hand still in his, gripping it tightly because I know that soon, he's going to pull away and leave.

He lifts my knuckles to his lips and kisses them before grinning like a madman. "You're welcome. That was really fun, actually. It's nice to have an outlet to get rid of all the shit I keep bottled up. When I'm with you, I find all sorts of outlets for my emotions."

"What shit do you keep bottled up?" I ask when we get to the passenger side of my car. Rather than get in and separate from his touch, I lean my back against it to keep him talking.

"Everything."

"Everything?" I repeat.

"Yeah, for years, it's felt like every time I start to figure out where the puzzle pieces of my life go, they all get tossed around again. It's so fucking frustrating!" he tells me, reaching up to tug on his hair with his free hand while still holding mine. "But then, being here with you just feels...right, like the pieces are easily falling into place without me trying."

"It feels like that for me too," I agree. "Even though we haven't known each other long, I think I already know you."

Letting my hand go to cup my face in between his hands, Maddox says, "You're the first person to see the real me, so thank you," before he brushes a soft kiss over my lips.

The night air swirling around us is heavy and charged, like right before a storm, as our eyes stay locked on each other. The way Maddox looks at me and makes me feel is both terrifying and invigorating.

"Do you maybe want to come back to my apartment tonight?" I ask, breaking the silence and bracing myself for his rejection.

"Hell yes," he actually agrees instead. "I'm so damn tired, I could pass out standing right here."

Oh.

Sleep is not exactly what I had in mind, but I'll gladly take every minute I can get with him.

"Then, let's go. I'll drive us back," I tell Maddox before I give him another quick kiss and then slip away from him.

CHAPTER SEVENTEEN

Maddox

I didn't plan on collapsing into Audrey's bed and falling asleep as soon as we walked in the door, but that's what happened.

It felt nice to be back in her room, surrounded by her warmth and her sweet scent. Hell, I even missed Stella, who curled up at my feet before I crashed, exhausted from the days without sleep and the beating I put on the professors.

Waking up with Audrey in my arms again feels perfect. I love the way she reaches for me in the dark, like even when she's unconscious, she knows I'll keep her safe and take care of her. It's a heady feeling I'll never get tired of.

Except, I can't get used to it either.

I'm days away from patching into the Savage Kings, and now I get why War kept Ren and Audrey away from the MC. I can't even imagine how devastating it would be if one of the club's enemies went after her...

"Holy shit!" I exclaim, as I jackknife into a sitting position in her bed.

"What's wrong?" Audrey asks as she sits up beside me, her bleary eyes trying to blink open.

Unfortunately, she's still fully clothed, like I am, since I was too tired to get undressed last night. At least she put on her pajamas.

"Nothing's wrong. I just had an idea, one that will help the club," I explain. "All thanks to you."

"Me?" she asks. "How's that?"

"I would do anything for you." I reach for the side of her face to bring her mouth to mine. "You know that, right?" I ask, as I keep feathering kisses over her lips.

"Good to know," Audrey says against my lips, as her hands reach for my shoulders to push my cut down them. "Does that include making love to me right now?"

"Hell yes," I agree before I attack her, flattening her back on the mattress while she continues to undress me. Unable to wait another second before I strip her naked too, I kiss my way down her neck and to her stomach before tugging her bottoms down.

"Maddox?" she asks, her tone serious.

"Yeah?" I ask, pausing with my mouth on her belly button.

"Will you come back, even if there's no one's ass to kick?"

"I don't think I could stay away from you if I tried," I reply honestly, knowing I should. Fuck, I should leave right now and never come back.

But at this moment, not even the threat of War could drag me away from her bed.

...

Audrey

WHILE MADDOX and I were sleeping, something changed between us.

And it's not the sex.

We'd had sex so many times those three days that I lost count, each time even hotter than the last. But this time is...different.

Maddox's mouth between my legs isn't just stroking the fires of pleasure to make me orgasm. It's possessive and dominating, with an intensity I've never felt before. He's owning me.

That much becomes even more obvious after a scream rips from my throat and my eyes roll back in my head.

Maddox's mouth crashes down on mine as he invades me. The weight of his body presses down on me, so he's the only thing I can see or feel. And I want all of him.

Our kiss breaks only because we're both struggling to get air in our lungs. But Maddox doesn't let up an inch anywhere else. He's inside me and covering me from head to toe, his forehead resting against mine as he watches my face. One of his palms is planted next to my head to hold just enough of his body off me so that I can still breathe while he rocks into me with slow but deliberate strokes that I never want to end.

"You feel that?" he asks. "It's perfect because you were made for me and only me."

"Yes." I dig my fingers into his shoulders to pull him closer, even though it's impossible. "Don't stop," I say, meaning more than this moment.

"How could I stop the best thing I've ever had?" Maddox asks with a grin before he swoops down and covers my lips with his. Our tongues dance while our bodies join in the same rhythm that doesn't falter until a wave of euphoria has my thighs tightening around Maddox's body wedged between them, and my pussy clamps down on his hard length to try and milk him dry, desperate to soak up his seed.

But that doesn't happen.

While my body is still shuddering, Maddox rears back and then takes himself in his hand, pumping his shaft until his thick release coats my stomach and between my breasts, marking me as his.

"Jesus," he grumbles before he collapses on top of the mess he just made and places kisses on my jaw. "You are incredible."

"*We're* incredible," I amend, then ask the question that's been on my mind ever since I saw him last night. "When are you coming back?"

"I need to get going after we get a shower," he says, pushing himself up to look at me better. "But I'll try to come back tonight."

"Good," I reply with a smile, liking how he said we would get a shower, meaning together. "I can't wait."

"Me either," he says.

CHAPTER EIGHTEEN

Maddox

I'M NOT WALKING INTO THE SALVAGE YARD—I'M PRACTICALLY floating.

And not just because Audrey and I fucked three times before I left her apartment, but because she's fucking amazing and I can't wait to see her again. Hopefully tonight, if all goes well with the snitch.

Even the phone call she got from War while I was inside of her the last time this morning couldn't bring down my good mood. She told him she was doing cardio, which wasn't exactly a lie.

I'm whistling a happy tune when I walk into the garage where Mike is still tied to the chair, looking like he's about to die.

"What's got you in such a jolly mood?" Miles asks, as he stands up from his metal chair and stretches his arms over his head, working out the kinks. "Guess that's because you weren't stuck here all night."

"Nope," I agree with a smile. I'm hoping my idea works, and no one will have to stay here tonight with the shithead. "I think Mike is finally going to tell us everything we want to know."

"How's that?" Miles asks. "We've threatened to cut or burn every appendage, and he won't budge."

"You haven't been focusing on the right body part," I tell him.

"Oh yeah?" he huffs. "What have we missed?"

"His heart," I reply.

The idea hit me when I woke up this morning with Audrey in my arms and the notion of doing anything for her was cemented inside of me.

"Oh, Mike..." I pull out my phone as I stroll over to stand in front of the abused man. I locate one of the photos from where I followed him, staying out of sight while we were still vetting all the guys, and then show it to him.

"Is this your girl? She's a pretty one," I say, causing his hanging head to pop up, eyes bulging in fear. "And look, there's her license plate number in the shot too. I bet Reece could get an address for her quicker than Miles can snap his fingers."

"Snap," Miles says, as he rubs his fingers together.

"Kim doesn't know shit, I swear!" Mike exclaims, finding energy and enthusiasm he didn't have just moments ago. "You can't hurt her!"

Of course the Kings wouldn't hurt her. But that doesn't mean I can't bluff that they will.

"Miles, call Reece and give him the plates," I instruct like I'm in charge here, because it suddenly feels like I am.

"On it, brother," Miles replies, as he pulls out his device and then puts it up to his ear.

Whether or not he's really calling him, I'm not sure, until I hear the ringing and then Reece's clipped, one-word answer. "What?"

"Mad Dog is back and working over our snitch," Miles says into the phone. "And we have a license plate for you to run..."

"No! Please," Mike begs as he fights against the binds and makes the chair legs come off the ground. "I'll tell you everything, just don't sic the Kings on her! Please! She's pregnant, goddammit. *Pregnant!*"

"You better talk fast," I tell him, then to Miles, "North Carolina plate, C as in Charlie..."

"The cops pulled me over the day I got my cut!" Mike starts jabbering. "I didn't do shit, but I had some weed on me. They held me for hours!"

"And?" Miles prompts, still holding the phone to his ear.

"My girl Kim was with me. We just found out we're going to have a baby. But Kim, she's not here legally. They were going to deport her, her and my baby, right then and there. Lock me up and ship my girl off. Then this woman came in, said she was with the ATF and could give me a clean record, make this all go away if I gave them information."

"What was her name and what did you tell her?" I ask.

"P-Peyton. Peyton Bradley. And all I told her were names of members, who hung around, and what they looked like. That's it, okay! I didn't give them shit! I didn't give them shit, and you can't hurt her, you fucking hear me!" Mike screeches.

"You would have, though," Miles says. "Eventually."

Now tears have sprung up in his eyes and are starting to overflow down his cheeks. "No, I swear! None of this was supposed to happen!"

"You hear that, brother?" Miles asks into the phone then gives me a side-eye. "Yeah, Mad Dog came through. Okay. Later," he says, before closing the burner phone and slipping it back into his pocket. "Now, it's time for the good stuff."

"What's the good stuff?" I ask in concern.

"Cut him loose," Miles instructs on the way to the door. "Make sure he cuts ties with the ATF, and then is out of the state within an hour. Then, you need to get your ass to the clubhouse."

"You don't want me to kill him, do you?" I ask.

"Would you?" he questions.

"If Torin told me to," I reply.

"Good answer, but no. Cut him loose. The little shit gave us what we need, and he gave us his reasons. Now, he better run for his life."

"Okay," I reply with an exhale. I didn't want to have to kill a man, but I think I could if I had to.

...

An hour later, I'm walking into the Savage Asylum after Mike put me on speaker so I could hear him call it quits with the feds and tell them he's moving to California with his girlfriend who he promised would be applying for her Visa. I think he meant it too because he blanched after he said it, like he didn't want me to know where they were headed. Then, I followed them to the airport with the promise that they wouldn't leave the terminal, unless it was on a plane across the country.

"The Kings are looking for you," Cedric says with a cringe when I walk past the bar.

"Which one?" I ask, concerned, since I was doing what Miles told me to do.

"*All of them*," Cedric whispers. "They're downstairs in the chapel. You better hurry because they looked pissed!"

"Shit," I mutter before I punch in the code and then hightail it through the basement to the open chapel door, tossing my phone into the box on the floor outside as I go.

"Sorry," I tell the guys, when I walk in the room and they're all seated in their chairs. "Mike called the agent and ended things. Now he's at the airport, catching a plane as we speak."

"Shut the door," Torin barks, completely ignoring my news, his face grimmer than I've seen it in months. Fuck, whatever is going on, it's not good. Are they pissed I threatened to hurt Mike's girl? Because I wouldn't.

"You got the name of the ATF agent?" War spins around in his chair to ask.

Swallowing past the knot in my throat, having to look him in the eye after sleeping with his sister again, I say, "Yes, Peyton Bradley. I heard her say so when she answered the phone."

Instead of responding, War nods silently, then gets to his feet and stands behind the chair. Tipping his chin up at the seat, he says, "Sit."

"Sit?" I ask as I glance around the table at the faces of the other members, who look equally pissed and closed off.

"Don't make me repeat myself," War threatens, so I walk over and lower myself into his chair, bracing my forearms on the table for whatever comes next.

"Take your cut off," Torin instructs from his seat at the head of the table. Before I can panic that I'm being kicked out, he lifts up another black leather cut from his lap and lays it flat on the table. "Replace it with this one."

"Holy shit," I mutter when I see the words "Savage Kings" on the patches above the bearded skull king with "North Carolina" underneath. "That's mine?"

"That's yours, *brother*," Torin says before his face finally breaks into a grin.

War's hands come down hard on my shoulders when he says, "Welcome to the table, brother," and then peels the prospect cut off my shoulders. "You've earned your spot through loyalty and devotion. Now you're a Savage King until you die or can no longer ride."

"Wow, thank you," I say, as I pick up the new cut and hold it in front of me, speechless because it's finally happening. Vaguely, I accept more congratulations, backslapping hugs, and fist bumps from the rest of the Kings.

My brothers.

War leaves and then comes back with another chair he pulls up to the table in the space to my left. Glancing over at me, he says, "Get comfortable because it's time for your first meeting."

"About the shit with the feds?" I ask.

"Yep," he replies.

"Now that we've got the name of the ATF agent investigating us, what are we gonna do?" I ask the table.

"We can't kill her or hurt her," Miles says. "If she goes missing, that'll just draw more attention to the club."

"And hurting women is *not* what we do," War mutters while glaring at Miles.

"War's right," Torin agrees. "So, how the hell are we going to handle this? Are we just gonna sit back and wait for Agent Bradley and the feds to bust in here to arrest us all, for who the hell knows what?"

"We need to find what she has on us," Chase speaks up and says. "If there's any evidence, we'll at least be able to hire attorneys to get in front of it."

"Reece, any chance you can work your magic on the computer to find out the details?" Torin asks.

He shakes his head. "Nope. Already tried. I can't get past any big government firewalls unless I'm on one of their internal devices. But what I *have* found out is that this ATF bitch has been pulling public arrest records off the databases, specifically Chase, Abe, Miles, and Ian's. There was also a hit on Sax's marina records and boat license files."

"Dammit," Sax grumbles. "If they bust me for the shit I do for the MC out in the Atlantic, I could get slapped with a life sentence."

"No doubt. Keep your boat in the docks except for recreational purposes until we know more," Torin orders.

"What about a laptop?" Dalton asks. "Could you hack into their system with a government-issued one?"

"Possibly," Reece agrees.

"If Agent Bradley has one that she brings home, I can lift it," Dalton confidently assures the guys at the table.

"*You?*" Chase asks with a *humph* of disbelief.

"Yeah, me," Dalton replies. "If she's looking into the Kings, she's seen the mugshots of half our guys and probably has all the military records too. Maddox was the main contact for her CI we busted, so he's out. Sax needs to lay low, which means that I'm the only one without a criminal history or dog tags."

"How is it possible that your dumbass has never been arrested?" Abe asks him.

"Do I look like a fucking outlaw?" Dalton responds with his arms spread out by his sides.

"Fuck no, blondie," Abe mutters. "Without any visible tats, you look like a California pretty boy who wears leather like it's a fashion statement."

"Exactly!" Dalton says, not looking the least bit insulted. Gesturing to his face, he says, "This is my 'get out of jail free' card. I can use my ridiculously good looks to grab this chick's laptop, no problem."

Torin snorts before turning to Reece and asking, "Do you think *Zoolander* here can really pull this off?"

"If I were a male model, I would be more like Hansel or Meekus," Dalton points out with a grin.

Reece rolls his eyes but eventually says, "Maybe, if he doesn't get caught."

"I won't get caught," Dalton assures the guys.

"All right," Torin says. "Then Reece, if you can get an address on this agent, I want you to go with Dalton to Raleigh tonight to start doing some surveillance. See if his sticky fingers plan is feasible without getting the club in any deeper shit."

"Sure thing, boss," Reece agrees, then grumbles under his breath, "Lord help me."

"I refuse to lose this MC because some woman with a power trip and a badge put a target on us. All in favor of the club committing a federal theft to try and save the Savage Kings?" Torin asks.

"Yea!" the table agrees, myself included, voicing my very first vote as a member.

After Torin slams down the gavel, ending my first official meeting, War says, "There's one more piece of business to take care of. Come on."

LANE HART & D.B. WEST

All the brothers get up from the table to follow him, so I do the same.

Our herd of men in black leather go up through the bar. For the first time, I actually feel like I'm a part of the group, not just the fringe on the outside. It's an amazing fucking feeling.

We all file out of the bar's back door...where a big, beautiful, new black Harley sits, the glossy paint and chrome pipes twinkling in the sunlight.

Some of the guys whistle as they walk around the Street Glide and inspect her.

"A King wouldn't be caught dead on that piece of shit bike you pulled into town on," War says, when he comes over to where I'm still standing in the background. Holding out his fist, he says, "Now you're gonna ride in style."

"*Me?*" I ask in disbelief. "This is mine?"

"Yep."

What the fuck?

"War, man, you bought me a new Harley?"

With a smile and a nod, I swear the big guy's golden eyes even get a little glassy when he says, "Not only have you been loyal to the Kings, but you've been loyal to me, helping me and my family out when we were in a tight spot during the storm. This is the least I could do. You've earned it, *brother.*"

Earned it? He thinks I deserve for him to buy me an expensive fucking bike, after how I've stabbed him in the back?

Fuck me.

"I-I can't take this, War," I tell him, slipping my hands into my jeans pockets to keep from snatching the keys from him against my will.

"You can, and you will," War declares. "Take the damn thing."

"No."

"Man, what's wrong with you?" Sax asks, throwing an arm around my shoulders. Gesturing with a wave of his hand to the bike as if I haven't seen it, he says, "The man is offering you a sweet ride. Why would you turn that down?"

"Because I've been sleeping with his sister."

At first, I'm not sure if I just thought the truthful words or spoke them. But then the silence and gaping jaws of the men surrounding us make it clear the words really did fall out of my mouth.

"Whoa, kid. Are you trying to get yourself killed?" Torin asks when he jumps between me and War, who still hasn't moved an inch. I don't think he's even blinked.

"What the fuck did you just say?" War eventually asks through gritted teeth.

"Shit," I mutter before raking my fingers through my hair. "Look, you think I'm loyal, but I've been lying to you for weeks. And I can't do it anymore, not when you're offering me this beautiful bike. It wouldn't be right for me to take it without you finally knowing the truth." Taking a breath, I finally spit it all out, glad to get it off my chest. "Audrey and I didn't go to Raleigh during the storm. We stayed at her place and we, well, we slept together. A lot. And then the other day, and last night..."

"You slept with my sister!" War roars before his arms start flailing at Torin, trying to get to me, uncaring that hitting his president could get him excommunicated from the MC. He doesn't reach me, thanks to no less than four brothers jumping in to help Torin hold him back. *Barely.* "I'm gonna kill you!" he threatens.

"Mad Dog, get the hell out of here before he makes good on his threat," Chase suggests, as he uses both of his hands to try and hold down War's right fist.

"I want his cut! He's done!" War shouts. "Get him out of here before I pound him into the pavement!"

Slipping off my cut that I haven't worn long enough for it to even soak up any of my body heat, I fold it and go lay it on the seat of the beautiful new Harley.

"What the fuck are you doing, kid?" Reece asks as he comes up and grabs the cut, then shoves it against my chest. "You put this back on and give him some time to cool down..."

"No!" War shouts. "I want him gone!"

"You don't get to make that decision just because you're pissed off, brother," Reece calls out to War, who's still being held back by half the members. "We've already voted him in."

"I don't give a shit!" War yells back, his face red with rage. "Get him out of here!"

"War, man, I get that you're angry, but you don't know what you're saying," Reece says. "And if you knew who he was—"

"Reece, don't!" I say, shoving the cut back at his chest to stop him before he outs me like this. I don't want to deal with the fallout of another lie I've been keeping, not right here and now. "It's fine. I'll go." I let the cut go, to hold up both of my palms up in surrender when I turn back to War. "But I love Audrey, maybe even more than this club," I tell him. "So, I don't give a shit what you say. You can kick me out of the MC, my apartment in the basement, and whatever else, but you can't make me stop seeing her."

"Like hell I can't!" he exclaims, the muscles in his neck bulging so severely that one's likely to rupture. "Leave my sister the fuck alone!"

"Sorry, but that's never gonna happen," I tell him before I turn and leave.

I hate walking away from the club, and all the men I've come to admire and respect, including my own blood, but I'm going to be with Audrey, even if I have to get to Wilmington on foot.

CHAPTER NINETEEN

Audrey

I wasn't all that surprised when Maddox called to say he was coming over.

What did catch me off guard was him asking me if I could come pick him up. The fact that he told me he would be walking down Highway Seventeen was also worrisome.

"Is everything okay?" I ask.

"I'll explain when I see you," Maddox tells me. "And I really need to see your face..."

"I'm on my way," I assure him, shocking myself because I didn't even feel the need to pull up the weather forecast and radar first to make sure no storms were on the way before heading out.

I made it to Hampstead before I came upon a lone figure walking toward me. It took me a second to even realize it was Maddox, since he wasn't wearing his typical black leather cut.

I pull over to the shoulder and he opens the passenger door to climb in.

"Hey," he says, leaning across the console to kiss me.

"Hey," I repeat when he pulls back, and then I see the fallen expression on his gorgeous face. "What's going on? Why are you walking? And where's your cut?"

"I got voted in today," he says blandly.

"To the MC? That's great, Maddox!" I reply, becoming confused when he doesn't share my enthusiasm. "Isn't patching in what you wanted? Why aren't you happy about that?"

"Because I couldn't lie to your brother anymore," he responds. "I told him about us."

My eyebrows shoot into my hairline because I didn't see that coming.

"You told War that we're seeing each other?" I repeat. "And I'm guessing he didn't take it well?"

"Nope."

Gasping in understanding, I say, "He kicked you out of the MC? I'll kick his ass!"

I start digging in my purse for my phone, but Maddox pulls my hand away and keeps holding it.

"It's fine," he says.

"It's not fine!" I argue. "The club means everything to you, and he has no right to act like my father..."

Giving my hand a squeeze, Maddox says, "I'm not going to stick around and cause more problems in the MC when they have enough shit to deal with. War can have the club as long as I still get you."

And my heart just melted into a little gooey pile in my chest.

"Oh, Maddox, are you sure?" I ask as I reach over to wrap my arms around his neck. "I know how much you wanted to be a King in the club your father built. Maybe you can have me and the MC both?"

"Can I stay with you for a while?" he asks as he continues to hold me tight.

"Of course," I tell him, pulling back enough to see his face. "I would love for you to stay and, as an added bonus, it'll drive Mindy crazy."

"I don't want to be a mooch. I'll get a job and help with rent..." he starts to say.

"I like having you around," I assure him. "And if you want to help out with rent, then I could finally boot Mindy."

"So, you would really want me to move in?" he asks.

"Yes!"

"Okay, thanks," Maddox replies. "Having to leave behind the MC was pretty devastating because it was all I had wanted for so long...but now, with you, my future is looking even brighter."

"Aww," I say before I reach for his face to kiss him again.

But despite his words, I know the loss of the Savage Kings cuts him deep, deeper than he will probably ever admit.

...

Maddox

OVER THE NEXT FEW WEEKS, my life transforms into something completely different than the past four years as I fall into brand new routines with Audrey.

She and War have had several arguments on the phone, but he hasn't come by her apartment to demand I leave, which has been a relief.

I was able to get a job as a valet for an uppity beach resort, making decent money in tips, and the best part was that I mostly worked during the day while Audrey was in class.

Occasionally, on my days off, I even go sit with her in Organic Chemistry to "observe" and remind the pervy professor to watch himself.

It only took about three days before I was successful in running off Mindy. She complained bitterly at first about our lovemaking keeping her awake. When we realized how much it aggravated her, we cranked it up an extra notch, until one afternoon, she was simply gone.

So yeah, things are going really great. I have an amazing girl, a nice place to live, and yet, there's still this emptiness inside me, like I'm missing out on an important part of my life.

I miss the MC and hate that I never had a chance to tell the guys, especially Torin and Chase, who my father was. I was hoping they could share stories about him with me, but now that's never gonna happen.

I can finally admit to myself I'm madly in love with Audrey, but the cloudy imaginings of the family I could have had with the Savage Kings casts a depressing shadow over me that never seems to break apart and blow away. Audrey notices when I get quiet and wistful, and always helps me by asking me to tell her about the brothers I had found in the MC, and reassuring me that if we just give Warren some time, he will definitely come around.

I can only hope she's right.

CHAPTER TWENTY

Maddox

"This isn't going to go well," I whisper to Audrey as we wait on the porch for someone to answer the door.

"You may be right," she agrees with a sigh. "That's why I'm ringing the doorbell instead of using my key to march right on in. We're making a united front and if he tells you to leave, then I'm going with you."

"You don't have to do that—" I start to say before the front door opens to reveal a scowling War.

"What the hell is he doing here?" War snaps.

"It's Thanksgiving and we're together," Audrey says, standing up to her much larger brother, not intimidated by his size in the least. Jabbing her finger into his broad chest, she says, "Warren O'Neil, other than Ren, I'm the only family you have left. And if you want to be a part of my life, then that means welcoming Maddox—"

"No," War interrupts her. "He's not stepping foot in my house."

The rejection stings, especially since I had come to think of War like a father during my years hanging around the club, and then prospecting with him as my sponsor.

"Go inside," I tell Audrey, and place my hand on her lower back to guide her.

A low growl comes from War when I touch her, but I ignore him. He doesn't need to scare me off. I get it, he doesn't want me around. Even though I'm not a hundred percent sure why he hates that I'm with Audrey so much, other than he doesn't think I'm good enough for her.

Well, I don't think I'm good enough either. But I'm trying my best to earn a living in Wilmington to support her now, and when we get married after graduation. Yeah, we've already talked about it and I can't fucking wait.

"Go eat dinner with your family and call me to come get you when you're ready to go," I tell Audrey.

"I want you to stay," she says, grabbing a fist full of my Henley tee and looking up at me with her sad, puppy dog eyes. "You're my family too."

"We'll have our own Thanksgiving dinner tonight," I promise her before I give her a quick kiss on the cheek, then quickly back away down the steps when War lunges toward me. "Just me and you, it'll be nice," I add.

"Are you sure?" she calls out as I walk around to the driver's side of her car.

"Yes, go. I love you," I yell back.

"Love you too," she replies, before blowing me a kiss that War interrupts when he grabs her arm and pulls her inside the house.

For the next few hours, I drive aimlessly around town before finally parking in one of the public beach lots. It's a little windy but a nice day, so I get out to go for a walk with my phone in my hand, debating whether or not I should call my mom.

Since Audrey has been nagging me to reach out to her, I finally take a seat in the sand dunes and dial the number for the house phone that I still remember by heart.

"Hello?" my mother answers.

"Hi, Mom," I reply.

There's a brief moment of silence. *"Maddox?* Is that y-you?" she eventually asks with a hiccup in her voice.

"Unless you have another son that you never told me about," I tease, to try and lighten the mood while blinking away the moisture gathering in my eyes. I'm pretty sure some sand blew into my face.

"Maddox! Where have you been? I just knew I was going to get a call when someone found you lying dead in a ditch!"

"I'm fine," I tell her. "I've been fine. I'm in Emerald Isle today, but I've been living in Wilmington for a few months now."

"What the heck are you doing on the coast?" she asks.

"This is where Deacon lived," I tell her.

"Oh."

"I've met some of the guys who knew him, and his two nephews. They're really nice."

I leave off the part about how they were so close to becoming *my* family before everything I wanted slipped from my fingers. Well, that's not exactly true.

"I met a girl and we're, um, living together," I inform her.

"Really? That's wonderful! I would love to meet her," my mother says.

"Audrey would really like to meet you too," I tell her.

"Then you should come home," she suggests. "I know you can't ever forgive me, but Todd and I forgive you. Now, he'll even tell you that he was selfish and deserved what you did to him."

"Is that right?" I ask, unable to believe he would ever say he deserved an ass whooping.

"We miss you, Maddox," she says. "Come home and see us. Please?"

Clearing the emotion from my throat, I tell her, "Yeah, Mom, we will. But Audrey's in college, so we'll have to wait until she finishes her classes."

"Of course," she agrees. "Anytime. You're our son. The door is always open."

"Thanks, Mom," I say as I heave a sigh of relief. It feels like a weight has been lifted from my shoulders after finally making contact with her. I was worried she would be angry at me or hell, have forgotten about me. But she hasn't.

...

Audrey

"YOU'RE BEING A REAL D-I-C-K, WARREN," I tell my brother, when the four of us sit down at the table in his dining room to eat Thanksgiving dinner without Maddox.

"D-u-c-k is duck, but I'm not allowed to say d-i-c-k," Ren informs me, making my jaw drop.

"He's reading now. Has been for a while," Warren says with a smile, reaching over to ruffle Ren's dark hair. Then, glaring at me, he says, "So don't spell anything else like that unless you want me to wash *your* mouth out with soap."

Rolling my eyes, I tell him, "I'm not a child anymore. Mom and Dad's threats no longer work on me."

"It was only a threat for you, the baby. But they actually *did* make me eat soap!" Warren grumbles.

"You deserved it for using the f-word on the church playground," I remind him.

"That little jerk knocked your teeth out. He's lucky all I did was call him a name and drag him by his collar over to his parents."

"It was a baby tooth, singular, so it wasn't a big deal," I explain to

Nova, who has been silently eating and observing our argument, which brings me to ask her, "Nova, what do you think about the situation with Maddox?"

"Oh no," she says, waving her white napkin at me like a flag. "I'm not getting in the middle of this."

"Good," Warren mutters.

"But I have met Maddox and I think he seems like a really nice young man," she adds, making me smile, and Warren turns to narrow his eyes at her.

"See!" I exclaim. "Maddox *is* a nice young man. And he loves me!"

"Whatever," my brother grumbles.

"He does!"

"You're too young to even know what love is," he replies.

"No, I'm not," I reply. "I remember how Mom and Dad looked at each other and how you could see the love between them. That's how I feel with Maddox. He's like the missing piece of my soul that no one else can fit."

"Maybe you should've majored in theatrics instead," Warren scoffs.

"Not only did Maddox come to Wilmington and help me when I needed him, but he gave up everything for me! You have no idea how much becoming a member of the Savage Kings meant to him. It was the one thing he's worked toward for *years*. All he wanted was to follow in his father's footsteps, with the only connection he had to the man, and you took that opportunity from him!" I say, then the words I just blurted out hit my own ears. I drop my fork and slap my palm over my mouth, wishing I could take them back.

"*His father's footsteps?*" Warren repeats because he was, unfortunately, listening to my entire rant, about the same time Ren asks, "What's the Savage Kings?"

"It's just a name of a group of men who ride motorcycles," my brother tells his son before turning to me. "What did you mean by *his father's footsteps?*"

"Nothing. Forget I said anything," I say in a rush before grabbing a roll and stuffing it in my mouth. "'Licious," I tell Nova around the mouthful.

"You're not supposed to talk with your mouth full," Ren helpfully informs me, and I give him a wink.

"Who is Maddox's father, Audrey?" Warren asks.

I take twice as long as usual to chew up the roll before I answer. "I have no clue what you're talking about."

My brother stares, unblinking, at me for several long moments before he tosses his own fork down with a clatter and pulls out his phone.

"War, really?" Nova asks, trying to deter him. "We're in the middle of Thanksgiving dinner. Can't you wait until later to make a phone call?"

"Nope, sorry," War tells her sweetly before his glare hits me with the force of a wrecking ball. "Reece," he says into the phone. "Who is Maddox's father?"

I hold my breath as I wait for some man on the other line to spill Maddox's secret that I promised him I would keep.

"No, I don't want to ask *him*, I'm asking you! You know, don't you?" Warren huffs. "It *is* my business! Don't you hang up on—" Warren pulls the phone from his ear to look at the screen. "He hung up on me!"

"Good," I say. "Serves you right for trying to be snooping in other people's business."

Instead of letting it go, my brother's head creases in thought. "Torin is way too young. And even Miles or Reece would've had to be, like, twelve, so that's rather impossible," Warren contemplates to himself aloud as he starts listing men. "So that leaves only the original members, and there's only three that Torin's really talked about. Eddie, who is still around, Rubin, who is Dalton's father, and Deacon, Torin and Chase's uncle."

"There are probably several others, right?" I quickly suggest when he gets too close.

Rather than respond to me, my brother gets back on his damn phone.

"Torin, hey brother, sorry to bother you on Thanksgiving," Warren starts. "Important question. If one of the original members had an illegitimate child of say, twenty-one years old, who would you guess is the father?"

"There is no way for him to know that!" I huff indignantly.

"Rubin or Deacon?" War says into the phone as he watches me for a reaction. "Yeah, I think it may be one of them too." It sounds like the man on the phone asks a question, to which War responds with a one-word response, "Maddox."

"Warren!" I exclaim. "This is none of your business, or anyone else's!"

Ignoring me, he says, "I've already called Reece and he won't tell me!"

"Hang up the phone, Warren!" I demand.

"I'm going to find out and when I do, I'll call you back," my brother says into the phone before he finally ends the call.

"I wasn't supposed to say anything, and it accidentally slipped out. Please, let it go," I beg.

"Fine, if you won't tell me, I'll just ask Maddox when he comes to pick you up," Warren declares.

"You would really do that?" I ask, as tears spring to my eyes. "You would ruin everything between me and Maddox because you're nosy and I almost let one of his secrets slip?"

"If it ruins everything, then you were never really in love, right?" the jerk asks.

The worst part is, I can't even argue with his logic.

CHAPTER TWENTY-ONE

Maddox

I CAN'T SAY I'M SHOCKED WHEN I PULL UP AT WAR'S HOUSE TO pick up Audrey, and he comes storming out with her on his heels. Fine, if he wants to hit me, I'll give him one shot. Maybe that will give him some sort of satisfaction.

Turning off the car, I get out and walk around to meet him in front of the hood.

"Who's your father?" he snaps at me.

"Huh?" I grunt, since I was expecting a physical blow, not a psychological one.

"Who is your father?" War repeats slowly. "Was he really a Savage King, or is that some bullshit you made up?"

"I'm sorry!" Audrey exclaims when she runs up beside her brother. I can tell by the pleading look on her concerned face that she must have accidentally spilled the beans. I'm sure she didn't do it on purpose, and I can't be mad at her for telling him my secret that I should've brought up a long time ago.

Figuring War wouldn't believe me if I simply tell him, I pull out

LANE HART & D.B. WEST

my wallet from my pocket and then remove the tattered old piece of paper that's been folded into a small square. "Here," I say when I offer it to him. "See for yourself."

"Maddox, you don't have to do this!" Audrey says, reaching between us and swiping the paper out of my hand before War. "I'm so, so sorry. I didn't mean to say anything, but I was angry at him and ranting, and when I was saying how much the Savage Kings meant to you, it just slipped out!"

"It's okay, baby," I tell her. Giving her a sad smile, I reach for her hand to pull her closer to my side. "Besides, it doesn't matter now."

"Are you absolutely sure?" She looks up at me with her big brown eyes.

"I'm sure," I reply before I gently remove my birth certificate from her fingers and hold it out to War again. He's so busy glaring at my other arm around his sister that it takes him a while before he finally snatches it from me.

Audrey and I watch silently as he unfolds the paper and then his eyes start to scan the words. When he gets to the important part, his golden eyes bulge before they lift to glance between the two of us again.

"Seriously?" he asks. "*Deacon* was your father?"

"According to my mother," I respond. "By the time I found out, he was already dead, so I couldn't ask him or get a DNA test. And while my mom lied to me about it for years, I don't think she would've put his name on my birth certificate unless she was certain," I explain. "She changed my last name from Fury to Holmes a few weeks later, when she married the asshole who raised me. My stepfather didn't want the inconvenience of having to deal with another man in our life..."

"Jesus," War mutters. "Why didn't you say anything before?"

"Why do you think?" I ask. "You and everyone else would've gone easy on me. I wanted to earn my patch, not just be handed one because of a name I was born with."

"So Torin and Chase don't know yet?" War asks.

"Nope."

"But Reece does?"

Nodding, I tell him, "Reece found my birth certificate and Change of Name documents when he was searching through my background. I asked him to keep it between us and told him that if I patched in, then I would tell everyone. So, he did."

"Wow," War mutters before he turns around and starts to walk back into the house. When he's a few feet away, he stops, remembering he's still holding my birth certificate. He comes back and hands it to me before disappearing inside.

Blowing out a breath, I tell Audrey, "It feels good to finally tell someone else."

"I feel awful," she says, burying her face against my chest.

"Don't. It's not a big deal," I assure her. "I was going to tell them...so now is as good a time as any."

Tilting her head back to look up at my face, she says, "My brother's a dick."

Smiling, I place a quick kiss on her lips. "He's just trying to protect you. Maybe you should tell him that you stole my innocence, and see if that helps his opinion of us being together," I tease.

"I will if you think it will help," she replies.

"No," I say, with a shake of my head. "Let's keep that embarrassing detail between us. I would never hear the end of it if the guys found out that a sweet little girl like you popped my cherry."

The smile slips from my face when I realize I won't be seeing the guys again to even give them a chance to rag on me. That part of my life is over.

Brushing that depressing thought aside, I decide to change the subject. "So, I called my mom today."

"You did?" Audrey asks excitedly. "How did it go? Was she happy to hear from you?"

"Yeah, I think so," I respond. "And she wants us to come visit..."

"Us?" Audrey repeats with a broadening grin.

"Yeah. Us. I told her about you."

"Aww, that's so sweet," she says, standing on her toes to kiss my lips. "I can't wait to meet her."

"I told her we would maybe visit when you finish up the semester."

"That sounds perfect," she replies. "Now, how about we go home and start our own Thanksgiving tradition?"

"That is a great idea."

CHAPTER TWENTY-TWO

Audrey

It's a week after Thanksgiving, when Maddox's phone rings while we're getting ready for bed.

"Must be work," he grumbles before he grabs it. His brow furrows seeing the screen. "It's Torin," he tells me before he answers. "Hello?"

I watch him as he listens, biting my lip because I already know what it's about.

Maddox doesn't know it yet, but my brother finally came through with what I consider an early Christmas present.

"Yeah, sure. Okay. See you then," Maddox says into the phone before he hangs up.

"What's up?" I ask innocently.

"Torin wants me to meet him at the salvage yard tomorrow afternoon," he says, face still showing his confusion.

"Did he say why?"

"No," Maddox answers. "And you don't exactly question the president...not that he's my president anymore."

"Right," I agree. "Well, come to bed. I'm sure it's nothing serious."

"Yeah," he agrees before he climbs under the sheets with me. "Mind if I borrow your car to drive up there?"

"Not at all," I respond before I push his chest down to the mattress to climb on top of him. "Now sit back, relax, and let me make you feel good."

A grin finally appears on his face. "You always make me feel good."

"Then I'm about to make you feel fucking amazing," I tell him as I start licking my way down his bare stomach. I glance up with a coy look. "Your birthday is coming up in twenty-two days, so do you want twenty-two spankings or twenty-two blowjobs?"

"Ooh, that's a tough one," he says, and then pauses as if he's actually considering his choice. "I think I'll go with...the blowjobs."

"I thought that's what you would say," I tell him as I reach down to wrap my hand around his hardening shaft and give him a squeeze before leaning forward to give the crown a thorough lick.

"Oh, yeah," Maddox groans, his eyes closing and hips rolling as his fingers thread through my hair. "Twenty-two days of this right here? You're too good to be true, baby."

"I'm gonna treat you better than a king," I promise him, before my lips wrap around his shaft and the time for talking is over.

...

Maddox

I honestly have no idea why Torin wanted me to meet him at the salvage yard. His voice didn't sound angry on the phone last night, and I can't think of anything I did wrong, so I'm thinking maybe he just wants me to return my key to the Savage Asylum and my apartment. He probably wanted me to do it in the salvage yard instead of the clubhouse to avoid War.

"Nice ride," Torin says from where he's casually leaning a shoulder against one of the open garage doors, when I climb out of Audrey's car.

"Haven't had a chance to come back and make the repairs on my old bike," I tell him as I approach. "Is that what this is about? You want me to get my shit out of the apartment and move my bike?"

"No," he responds. "We just wanted to talk to you."

"We?"

Jabbing his thumb over his shoulder, he says, "Chase is here too."

"Oh," I mutter as the other Fury brother comes out to join him. "I guess War told you?"

"He didn't come right out and say it, but we've put the pieces together enough to make a guess," Chase responds. "So, our Uncle Deacon was your father?"

"According to my mom," I answer, as I pull out my birth certificate and offer it to Torin. "They went to school together."

"And he didn't know?" Torin asks as he reads the paper and passes it to Chase.

"Nope. I didn't even know until six years ago."

"Why didn't you tell us?" Chase questions.

"Do either of you ever wonder if you got special treatment with the MC because of your uncle?" I ask.

"Deacon didn't go easy on us, that's for sure," Torin replies with a grin. "But yeah, it probably took Chase and me a little longer to actually earn the respect of the other brothers who thought we were given a free pass."

"That's what I thought," I say. "And I didn't want to have to wonder if I got my patch because of the name I was born with. I wanted to earn it."

Chase and Torin exchange a look. "Makes sense," Chase says. "A weaker man would've walked into the Savage Asylum on day one and posted *this* on the wall to try and take the easy way." He waves my birth certificate in the air before handing it back to me.

"Thought never crossed my mind," I admit. "Honestly, after meeting the two of you, I wanted to bury the damn thing or burn it because I was worried that if either of you found out, you would think I was trying to steal your MC or some shit."

"It's not our MC," Torin says. "And it's not War's either. We're all just one piece of a bigger brotherhood, and we voted you in unanimously."

"I know," I agree. "But War was there first, and I don't want to cause more problems for the club."

"You think you and War are the first brothers to have an argument?" Chase asks with a chuckle, then turns to his brother. "How many times have you and I fought?"

"Too many times to count," Torin remarks with a grin. "But we settle our shit and do what's best for the club. You willing to squash this shit with War?"

"Not if it means giving up Audrey," I say without hesitation.

"She's not a kid anymore, so War doesn't get a say in who she dates," Torin tells me. "It's been months, so I think he's willing to admit that now and move on."

"That's not what he said at Thanksgiving," I mutter.

"Your legacy was the slap in the face War needed to get his head out of his ass and remember what this club is about," Chase says. "So now it's your turn to decide if you're a Savage fucking King or not."

"I'm a King," I tell them with a grin.

"Good," Torin responds. Sweeping his hand inside the garage, he walks in further and says, "Your chariot awaits."

"I can't accept that bike from War," I say as I follow him, Chase right behind me.

"Understood," Chase agrees. "But you *will* take these bikes because they're classics, and Torin and I have enough Harleys to start another dealership."

"Wow," I say as my gaze lands on the restored beauties.

"These were Deacon's, so we couldn't get rid of them," Torin tells me with a slap on the back. "And it's a good thing too, because if he had known that he had a son, he would've wanted you to have them."

"Seriously?" I ask. "They were—"

"Your father's," Torin answers. "And you're probably going to get tired of us talking about him now..."

"Never," I assure him. "I want to know everything."

"We'll go all the way back to the beginning and *my* journey down the King's Road, when I first started prospecting," Chase says. "Deacon gave me my cut right after my eighteenth birthday, when Torin was still in the Army."

"So, you patched in before Torin?" I ask in surprise. "Why didn't you become president? No offense to you, Torin."

Chuckling, he says, "None taken. Chase was offered the gavel and he turned it down."

"Hell, I'm not president material and everyone has always known it," Chase responds. "But who knows, maybe you are."

"Me?" I repeat.

"Someone has to fill Torin's shoes one of these days," Chase points out.

"And you think that could be me?"

"You're smart, and you keep your anger in check, even though I'm guessing you probably inherited the Fury temper," Torin says.

"I've let it out a few times," I admit.

"Did they deserve it?" Chase asks with an arched eyebrow.

"Hell yes," I answer without hesitation.

"Then that's all that matters," he replies with a grin. "A leader has to keep a cool head when it counts. Not many of our brothers have that ability. Deacon always seemed so calm and in control. But one look at him and you knew that if he wanted, he could flip a switch and take on a giant if he needed to."

"He was a big guy?" I ask.

"And tough as nails," Torin responds. "He smoked a pack a day but could deadlift a truck."

"That's what killed him, right? He died from lung cancer?"

"Yep, right after I got out of prison," Chase says grimly. "He promised me he would hold on until I got out and he did, barely."

"That was one of the best things about him," Torin says. "Deacon was a man of his word. And too generous. If he told you he was going to do something, he did it. When I took over for him, the club's books were in the negative. He had overextended himself, and had to use his own money to pay all the charities and veterans he helped year after year."

"Sorry, but there's no inheritance, except for these bikes," Chase tells me.

"I don't care about that. I never came here for money," I explain. "I just wanted to know more about the man who was a missing piece of my life."

"We'll share as many pictures and stories as you can handle," Torin offers. "How about we head over to the bar and raise a beer to your old man?"

"Sounds good," I agree with a smile, anxious to try out one of my new bikes. These classics, I will graciously accept because they were my father's. I hope Deacon would've been proud of me, the man I've become, and the King I'm going to be.

CHAPTER TWENTY-THREE

Audrey

"CAN I HAVE EVERYONE'S ATTENTION?" MY BROTHER SHOUTS over the noise of the crowd and the thumping music. "I want you to all meet...my sister, Audrey."

Someone whistles and Warren glares in their direction. "She's with Maddox, so all of you need to keep your hands off of her!" he yells. "Oh, and girls, you better leave Maddox alone too. Messing with him is messing with my sister."

"Yes, Daddy!" one of the guys calls out in a falsetto, and I get to see one of the rare times my brother flips someone the finger in front of me. Maybe he really is ready to admit I've grown up.

"Thank you for inviting me," I tell Warren.

"Yeah, yeah. Whatever," he huffs before slipping an arm around Nova's shoulders. "You're not a child. Blah, blah, blah. I get it, okay?"

"I pity you, woman," I say to Nova. "How do you put up with my brother's constant need for control?"

Her cheeks turn rosy red before she says, "Oh, we've found a few...creative ways to help him let out his dominating side."

Nose wrinkling with disgust, I grumble, "Eww, now I wish I hadn't asked," right before the door to the bar opens. I turn around just in time to see two tall, tough-looking bearded men walk in... followed by Maddox.

Instead of yelling "Surprise!" there's a chorus of deep masculine whoops in celebration as my man stares in shock at the large gathering of people. Most are Savage Kings interspersed with scantily-clad women.

Elbowing my brother in his side, I hiss, "Go! Take him his cut."

"Fine," Warren grumbles before he removes his arm from Nova. He then reaches for the leather cut that's draped on one of the empty barstools. I follow him through the crowd that's gathered around to greet Maddox, most of the men offering him handshakes and back-slapping hugs.

"Here," I hear Warren say when he holds out the leather to Maddox. "Don't step into this clubhouse again without it."

"Yes, sir." Maddox starts to take the cut with a grin before his gaze drifts over Warren's shoulder and he spots me.

"Hey," I say, with a little wave of my fingers.

"Audrey!" Maddox looks from Warren to me several times with his jaw gaping. "What are you doing here?"

"I made my brother give me a ride on his Harley." I shoulder through to throw my arms around his neck. "Congratulations!" I tell him, placing a kiss to his cheek.

"You knew about all this?" he asks.

"I did," I agree with a broad smile.

I take the cut from my brother's hands, holding it up for Maddox to slip on.

"I can't believe you're here," he says as he puts one arm in and then the other.

When the leather is finally where it belongs, I run both of my palms over his chest that's now decorated with additional patches proclaiming him as a member. Seeing him wearing the cut again also reminds me of the first day we met. "This is a good look on you. I've missed it the last few months."

"Me too," Maddox agrees, covering my hands with his. "Are you sure you're okay with all of this?"

"She is," Warren speaks up before I can. "Trust me, I've tried my best to talk her out of it."

"You won't regret it," Maddox says with a kiss to my lips, even though I'm pretty sure he was talking to my brother as much as he was to me.

"I know I won't," I reply before I kiss him back, harder this time, and with enough tongue that I hear Warren mutter a curse.

He calls out, "Hurt her, and I'll kill you," then leaves us alone.

"You must be Audrey," a rumbly, authoritative voice says from beside us, followed by a chuckle. When I glance over at him, the bearded guy says, "And you may want that key back for a little longer."

He holds up a keychain dangling from his finger that Maddox snatches from him with a word of thanks.

"Congrats, brother," another younger guy, one covered in tattoos, says when he strolls up to us with a beer in his hand. "Let me know when you're ready to get your new ink."

"New ink?" I ask.

"The Savage Kings patches," Maddox responds. "And I can't wait," he tells the guy who I'm assuming must do the club's tattoos. "Any chance we could do it later tonight?"

"Absolutely," the man agrees. "We can get started, but it may take a few days to do your entire back."

"Actually, Gabe, man, if it's okay, I was thinking about putting mine here," Maddox says, flattening his palm on the left side of his chest. "Will that work?"

"That will look awesome, brother. I've used photos of the ink on all the original members to design the new ones. That's exactly where Deacon had his."

"No shit?" Maddox asks.

"Yeah, it was Chase who got the Kings' back tat trend started," Gabe responds. "But I'm all for something new."

"Thanks, Gabe," Maddox says, offering him a fist bump.

"Come over to the shop whenever you're ready," he tells him.

"We're probably gonna celebrate for a few hours first," Maddox says, pulling me closer.

"Understood," Gabe replies with a chuckle, then disappears back into the crowd.

"So how do you plan for us to celebrate for the next few hours?" I look up at Maddox's face.

"I think you can guess," he answers with a grin.

CHAPTER TWENTY-FOUR

Maddox

"Come on," I tell Audrey as I pull her by her hand over to the door that leads to the basement, once we get a chance to slip away.

"Where are we going?" she asks as I punch in the code and start down the steps.

"I want to show you where I've lived the last few years," I reply, looking over my shoulder at her when we get to the bottom. "And I can't wait another second to strip you naked and lick you from—"

"Just the man I was coming to see!" Reece's loud voice interrupts before I can finish my sentence. "Good to see you back here, brother! I saw you come in with Torin and Chase."

Turning to face him, I ask with a smirk, "You don't have cameras hidden in the apartments, do you?"

Scoffing, he says, "No, and it's not my fault if people decide to fuck in public places where my security cameras just so happen to be located. Speaking of which, hello, Audrey. Nice to finally meet you in person." Reece holds out his hand to Audrey, who takes it with her eyebrows raised in confusion.

"Reece handles the club's IT shit *and* he monitors the club's, um, perimeter," I explain to her.

"Oh, it's nice to meet you too," Audrey replies, then adds, "Ohhh," when it dawns on her he saw us when we got busy in the alley. I hadn't told her because I didn't want her to be embarrassed.

"Go find your own woman to do dirty things with instead of watching other people, old man," I tease Reece before I pull Audrey away and into my old apartment.

"He watched us?" is the first thing she asks when I shut and lock the door.

"Ah, yeah. I knew cameras were around outside, but I didn't think they would be right up on us. Sorry," I tell her.

"It's okay," she replies. "Guess the chance of getting caught or being watched by someone else is why sex in public is so fun."

"Yeah," I agree with a smile, glad that she's not upset. "You up for having a little fun in private?"

"God, yes," Audrey agrees as she moves in front of me and grips the opening of my leather cut in both of her hands. "But this time, I want you to keep this on."

"Done, baby," I easily agree since I wasn't ready to take it off just yet. Today seems almost too good to be true.

I've been given everything I've ever wanted, and more.

CHAPTER TWENTY-FIVE

Maddox

LATER THAT NIGHT, WHEN AUDREY AND I ARE BACK UPSTAIRS, War and Nova come over to our table in the corner and sit down with us. I've got a bottle of Jack Daniel's and a two-liter of Coke sitting in front of me. Once I pour Audrey and myself a fresh round, War picks up the bottle and takes a long pull.

"I didn't really get a chance to talk to you enough earlier," War says as he wipes at his lips.

"About what?" Audrey asks.

"Not you, him," War snorts. "Even with the birth certificate on Thanksgiving, I was still, I don't know, skeptical of everything..."

"You were being stubborn, and a bit of a d-i-c-k," Nova interrupts.

"Yeah, that too," War agrees. "Anyhow, I made Reece run your records again, you know, so I could see things for myself, and..." he trails off to take another pull from the bottle. "I saw a police report with your name on it, from when you two were down in Wilmington during the storm. Report says there were some looters in her building, and you fought them off and then turned them over to the Guard out there."

"Yeah, it was a crazy few days," I admit to him. "We should have told you about that too, but I just didn't know how to tell you about Audrey and I after…I don't know, man, after all you have been to me, you understand? You're the closest thing I've ever had to a real father, and I didn't want to disappoint you…"

"Disappoint me?" War scoffs. "When I read that shit, I was so damn proud of you. You took care of her, maybe not like I asked you too, but the best way that you could. She's just as stubborn as I am in her own way."

"Hey!" Audrey protests, kicking at War under the table.

"Keep your pointy-ass toes to yourself, woman," War snarls playfully before taking another drink. "I talked to Nova about it, and she convinced me to say…" War trails off, looking at Nova, almost helplessly.

"It's all right, you can do it. Spit it out, Warren," Nova reassures him.

With a heavy sigh, War says, "Reading that report made me realize that you belong here. Both of you. Audrey, you deserve the truth, from me, from Maddox, hell, from everyone in your life. And Maddox, boy…you deserve your place in the Kings and with my sister. You could ride a lot further and a lot harder, and I don't think you two would ever find a better match for each other. I'm glad you're together, even though I don't always like looking right at it."

As soon as he finishes talking, War gives a firm nod to Nova, then stands up from the table, the bottle of Jack Daniel's still clutched in his massive grip. "I'll bring another bottle," he mutters before he stomps away.

"Give him a minute." Nova smiles. "He needs to compose himself after getting all that off his chest."

"War!" I call out to him before he can get further away. When he turns around, scowling, I hold up Audrey's hand, our fingers intertwined. "Thank you, brother. From the bottom of my heart. Thank you."

Warren gives me another of his nods then turns away, but not before the overhead lights catch the shine of wetness in his eyes. He raises a hand to swipe at his face as he stomps off to the bar.

"Don't mention that when he comes back," Audrey cautions me.

"I wouldn't dream of it," I snort.

I keep half my attention on the big man as he stands by the bar, noticing that Reece walks over to him and leans in close to speak with him. When War turns to come back to the table, he jerks his head for Reece to follow him over. Reece pulls up a nearby empty chair, then sets his beer on the table as he sits down with us.

"Well, this is unusual." I grin at Reece. "To what do we owe the pleasure of your company this evening? What brings you up out of the dungeon?"

Reece sits up and cranes his neck to look around the crowded bar, then turns back to us with a slight frown. "I was just asking around to see if anyone had seen Cynthia. I've been kind of busy dealing with some things with Dalton, and just realized I haven't seen her in a few days."

"*You* are looking for Cynthia?" I ask in surprise.

Thinking that I don't know exactly who she is, he starts describing her. "Tall, wavy red hair, kind of..." Reece trails off and flushes slightly as he looks between Audrey and Nova, then mumbles, "Kind of stacked, I guess is a polite way to say it?"

"Is this Cynthia your girlfriend?" Audrey asks, causing War to snort as he takes another shot of Jack, then starts coughing violently.

Reece reaches over and pounds War on the back a few times, until his spluttering cough turns into laughter. "Cynthia is everybody's...friend, and nobody's girl," War finally manages to choke out.

"War! That's terrible," Nova protests, even though she grins slightly as she looks around at some of the club's other ladies. "I take it she's one of the, uh, regulars?"

Reece nods, and says, "Yeah, she's been hanging around for a while now, looking for an old man, I guess."

"You thinking about filling that position?" I ask him pointedly.

"No," Reece protests, a bit too quickly and loudly in my ear. "I'm just...I'm supposed to look out for threats to the club, and if something has happened to her, it's important I find out what, that's all."

"Well, you were going to run that plate number for Mike's old lady the other day. You're bound to have this girl Cynthia's, if she ever drove over here. Could you try to track her down?" I ask him.

"I was hoping it wouldn't come to that." Reece sighs. "It feels...I don't know, like I'm being a stalker or something. I guess I don't have much choice, though, if she doesn't show up tonight."

"When has feeling like a stalker or a Peeping Tom ever bothered you?" Audrey asks, this time, making *me* snort and choke on my drink. If War ever heard about that incident in the alleyway, god help us all!

Audrey and I both burst into laughter, while War and Nova just look at each other and shrug, obviously not concerned about whatever the inside joke might be. As soon as I recover, I try to steer the conversation away from *that* particular topic as quickly as possible. "Yeah, man, stalking is kind of your thing. Why would you feel bad about doing it to Cynthia?"

"No reason, no reason at all," Reece replies, unconvincingly. "You know what, I'm going to go get to work on that right now. You guys have a good night."

Reece stands up, grabbing his beer and rapping his knuckles once on the table.

"You too, Reece," Audrey says sweetly. "Go get your girl!" she adds to his back, causing him to flip us the bird as he heads for the stairs to the basement.

"There's something weird going on there," War observes once Reece disappears. "I don't think I've ever heard him ask about a woman."

"Well, if he needs anything, we'll be here for him," I say, as I raise my glass to War. "But on the way over here tonight Torin told me that my father used to have a saying that I think is appropriate right now. Deacon used to say, 'don't try to tackle tomorrow's problems today.' That sounds like good advice to me."

"True words, brother," War agrees as he clinks his bottle against my glass in toast. "Enjoy your evening, Maddox. And welcome to the family. Both of them."

EPILOGUE

Maddox

"ARE YOU READY?" I ASK AUDREY WHEN I TAKE HER HAND in mine.

"No. Yes. No!" she responds with a wince. "Maybe?"

"It's gonna be okay, baby. I promise. Trust me?" I ask, placing a kiss on her forehead.

"Yes," she agrees, taking a deep, steadying breath.

"Okay, on the count of three?" She nods so I start the countdown. "One. Two. Three."

On three, I push open the door to Audrey's apartment complex with my left hand and then pull her out onto the sidewalk, into the drizzling rain. There's no thunder or lightning, I made certain of that. Otherwise, I wouldn't risk bringing her out.

"Ah!" Audrey screams in what sounds like both fear and excitement all at once. She tilts her face up to the sky, letting the droplets of water wash over her while still squeezing my hand hard enough to fracture bones. "I did it! I'm standing in the rain!"

"You did it," I agree, thinking she's the most beautiful woman I've ever seen standing out here, trusting me enough to let me help her face her biggest fear.

But my plan isn't finished yet.

Hopefully, I'll not only prove to my girl that she's safe in the storm, but also give her a better, happy memory to hold onto in the future.

I reach into my leather cut and pull out the small black ring box then kneel down in a puddle in front of her, still holding her left hand.

"Audrey O'Neil, I risked life and limb to get your brother's permission to ask you this, but he gave it to me, so will you do me the honor of becoming my wife?"

"Yes!" she exclaims.

Thank god. Unable to wait another second to see her wearing my diamond ring, I pull it out of the box with my teeth and toss the box to the sidewalk so I can slip it on her finger.

"Holy shit, yes!" Audrey says again as she examines her left hand, then tugs me up to my feet to kiss me.

I hold her in my arms and kiss her back until a few minutes later, when Audrey pulls away. "Oh my god. I forgot it was even raining!"

"You're doing great, baby. I'm so proud of you," I tell her, reaching up to push the damp hair out of her face. "And I can't fucking wait to marry you."

The two of us have talked about marriage for months, but it wasn't official until now, with her wearing my ring and saying the word after I officially had War's permission. I would've married her without it, but I'm happy her brother approves.

Now, both of our families will get to be at our wedding, hers and mine.

The father I never met won't get to celebrate with us, but my Savage Kings brothers will all be there, making it feel like Deacon's spirit is not only alive, but always watching out for me, no matter where the road takes me.

The End

COMING SOON!

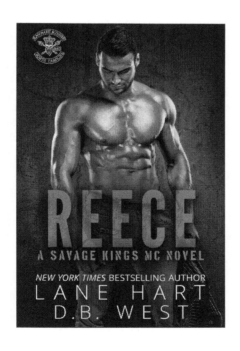

Reece's book is coming in March!
Pre-order now!

ABOUT THE AUTHORS

New York Times bestselling author Lane Hart and husband D.B. West were both born and raised in North Carolina. They still live in the south with their two daughters and enjoy spending the summers on the beach and watching football in the fall.

Connect with D.B.:

Twitter: https://twitter.com/AuthorDBWest

Facebook: https://www.facebook.com/authordbwest/

Website: http://www.dbwestbooks.com

Email: dbwestauthor@outlook.com

Connect with Lane:

Twitter: https://twitter.com/WritingfromHart

Facebook: http://www.facebook.com/lanehartbooks

Instagram: https://www.instagram.com/authorlanehart/

Website: http://www.lanehartbooks.com

Email: lane.hart@hotmail.com

Join Lane's Facebook group to read books before they're released, help choose covers, character names, and titles of books! https://www.facebook.com/groups/bookboyfriendswanted/

<u>Find all of Lane's books on her Amazon author page!</u>
Sign up for Lane's newsletter to get updates on new releases and freebies!

Made in the USA
Las Vegas, NV
01 November 2021